5x 2/11 ˅12/11
5 4, 12/11 - 3/12

BETWEEN TWO SEAS

Carmine Abate

BETWEEN TWO SEAS

*Translated from the Italian
by Antony Shugaar*

Europa
editions

Europa Editions
116 East 16th Street
New York, N.Y. 10003
www.europaeditions.com
info@europaeditions.com

Copyright © 2002 by Arnoldo Mondadori Editore
This edition published in arrangement with Grandi & Associati
First Publication 2008 by Europa Editions

Translation by Antony Shugaar
Original Title: *Tra due mari*
Translation copyright © 2008 by Europa Editions

Library of Congress Cataloging in Publication Data is available
ISBN 978-1-933372-40-2

Abate, Carmine
Between Two Seas

Book design by Emanuele Ragnisco
www.mekkanografici.com

Printed in Italy
Arti Grafiche La Moderna – Rome

CONTENTS

BETWEEN TWO SEAS

to Meike, naturally
a Meike, naturalmente
natürlich für Meike
ne, Meikes

DEPARTURE

W hat did I know about him? One day in July, he was arrested, and he vanished from my life for years without anyone ever bothering to tell me his story. I was just a child. What little I knew was all lies, and as time passed I forgot them.

There were times, though, when a yearning crept up on me as I slept; I would follow an echoing, distant voice and then, unexpectedly, tumble into the emptiness of night and come gliding down, drenched in sweat, down to his village. I heard his first and last name spring up like a gust of wind in the piazzas or in the bars and cafés: "Giorgio Bellusci!" There, once again, was his thuggish gaze. The warmth of his enormous hands. And most of all, my love for him, because you can forget a man like Giorgio Bellusci all you want; in the end, he comes back to life on you, more overpowering than ever.

"Welcome, Florian," he would say, planting a kiss on my forehead. And then he'd vanish again.

Beyond the Fondaco del Fico, toward the sea, the eye encounters nothing but clayey hills, stands of Holm oaks, and ravines cluttered with briers and brambles. On all sides stretch withered, waterless low mountains, like heaps of cattle dung deposited here and there. The road that climbs up to my mother's village looked as if it had been ravaged in a bombing raid, a cracked serpentine road riddled with zigzagging arrays of deep potholes. Our Volvo station wagon chugged and huffed up the steep grade, in the stifling heat. My father drove, tense and impatient; perhaps he was even unhappier than I was, but he said nothing.

I had held out since Hamburg, all the way to the exit ramp off the superhighway, 2,581 kilometers of boredom and discomfort, like a bee caught under an overturned glass, always last in a long line of cars, all of them charging along faster than us, rushing past the endless ranks of blossoming oleanders. But that final stretch of road was the most vomitous of all, in the sense, that is, that it sometimes made me vomit.

I was arriving for the long holidays, and already I was eager to turn around and leave.

The village sits like a horseshoe on a hill between two seas, the Ionian and the Tyrrhenian. It has a pretty name—Roccalba, "white fortress"—but I scornfully pronounced it Roc-calda, "hot fortress," because of the mantle of muggy airless heat that weighs mercilessly upon it all summer long.

Every two minutes, my mother would announce: "*Klaus, Florian, wir sind gleich da!*" and point out a thistle still in bloom or the season's first figs, the greengage plums, or pomegranates already split open by the heat, gleeful like someone about to be ushered into paradise. My father stared straight ahead like a shipwrecked sailor, eyes peeled for the rusted sign bearing the name of Roccalba. His face only broke into a smile once he set foot in the village, and he never let that forced smile relax for the rest of the holidays. My mother, on the other hand, was genuinely overjoyed. She would set eyes on her parents again, her sister Elsa, her niece Teresa, her childhood friends, the narrow lanes, the pens full of newborn pigs, the crickets in the olive trees, the gullies behind the church, the variegated chrysanthemums on the balconies, the swallows wheeling overhead in the vast sky. "Have you ever seen a sky so big, Florian?" she would ask, though she knew I'd never answer. "At night you can see every star in the firmament, down to the sea, out to infinity." Finally, she would again set eyes on the Fondaco del Fico. Her father, Giorgio Bellusci, took her out there in the late morning hours: the two of them, alone in the heat, in the middle of the countryside, sat talking animatedly after a year's separation, before the ruins of the ancient family inn, once the most famous establishment in all Calabria, as she boasted.

"Yes, maybe so, but now it's just an eyesore, a shabby look-ing wall of scorched stones, overgrown with briers and wild fig trees," Elsa's husband, Uncle Bruno, said one evening, tact-lessly trying to knock her off her high horse. My mother instantly flew into a rage, attacking him with a fusillade of words: "Simple-minded ignorant hick, you think you know something about the history of our Fondaco? You know how to stuff yourself with food, is all you know." We were just fin-ishing dinner. Giorgio Bellusci, on the other hand, kept his temper; in fact, he grinned in amusement. Then, taking careful aim at Uncle Bruno's right eye, he spat a rapid volley of water-melon seeds that hit their mark with a splat. "There's an eye-sore for you," he finally announced, with solemnity. We all burst into laughter, even Aunt Elsa and her daughter Teresa, everyone except Uncle Bruno, who glared at his brother-in-law, with one eye smoldering and the other smeared with spit and watermelon seeds. But we all understood that the remains of the Fondaco del Fico demanded respect, like those of a deceased relative. And that soon enough Giorgio Bellusci would bring them back to life.

Yes, more than anything else, I knew this about him: he loved the Fondaco del Fico the way you love a family member, maybe more. And that he was my mother's father—my grand-father. He was in many ways a warm and caring man, but I could never bring myself to call him Grandpa, perhaps because I'd always seen him only one month each year, and even then almost exclusively at meals. Ever since the time he vanished without even saying goodbye, a resentful indifference had been smoldering inside me. I told myself I cared nothing about him, because he cared less than nothing about me. Never a letter or a postcard; never a phone call to say hello. It was as if he had been swallowed up forever by the muggy sea of heat that washed over Roccalba the summer of his arrest.

Fortunately, just as the gap separating us was becoming unbridgeable, I learned about the journey he took in his youth. At first from my mother, then from my grandmother, and later from Hans Heumann and his photographs. I was a boy; the first time, I listened apprehensively. At times, I broke out in a sweat. "The village stank of summer," my mother began the story, and I felt as if I were listening to the echo of a song I'd heard who knows when, an echo that still follows me everywhere, like a chorus of invisible crickets or furious swallows. Suddenly, I saw Giorgio Bellusci in a clear new light; I could make out his footprints in the dust, and I seized onto him with all my strength.

FIRST JOURNEY

The village stank of summer. The muggy heat clung to the skin like hot glue, but Giorgio Bellusci set off on his journey all the same. Not even an earthquake could have stopped him, not even cannon fire. He set off on his journey to a city he knew nothing about, only the name—Bari—and the direction in which it lay: north, somewhere beyond Metaponto, on the shores of a sea called the Adriatic. On a street in this city there lived a pretty girl named Patrizia Cassese, who vacationed for a month every winter with her family in Camigliatello, in a cottage they owned, surrounded by fir trees and chestnut trees and snow. It was there that she had met Giorgio Bellusci, in a trattoria in Camigliatello; he was a regular customer, as he spent all summer in the surrounding countryside with his herds of cattle, and he had more friends there than in Roccalba.

He had just turned twenty-two, and his parents—understanding the stubbornness that ran in his veins—knew better than to try to talk him out of going. Instead, they hugged him tight in the presence of all their neighbors, who murmured in chorus: "That boy is crazy; up there, if he ever gets that far, the brothers and the father this Patrizia will eat him alive"; overlooking the fact that Patrizia had no brothers, and that her father, city-born and city-raised, wasn't a jealous relic like they were. After that, his parents locked themselves behind a façade of pride, and, not a moment after he set off on a Vespa loaded with food and flagons full of water and wine, they sat down to await his return.

Giorgio Bellusci rode through the countryside of Roccalba, suffocating in the damp heat of August, as if he were passing through a restless early-morning dream. On his left, toward the dry riverbeds, he glimpsed the ruins of the Fondaco del Fico. His foreboding grew until it became intolerable. He tried to ward it off by singing a little ditty, by gulping down a couple of mouthfuls of wine, by barking out a loud laugh that startled the birds and the crickets. It was no good. His foreboding continued to grow. And so he twisted the throttle to make the Vespa go at top speed, shouting as if death were at his heels.

It was not until he saw the sea glittering on his right that calm and contentment returned. And for the first time since leaving, he thought of Patrizia: she might already be engaged or even married; she might not even care for him anymore. The trip was a fool's errand; he knew that. With all the beautiful, respectable, wellborn girls to choose from in Calabria, he had to go all the way to Bari? A senseless journey is what it was, and he was a lunatic—everyone in Roccalba said the same thing: brides and bovines from your hometown. Yet, he could feel the urge to leave growing within him, and he almost felt that the others in town envied him.

Evening had fallen; it was late. He dismounted from the rattletrap Vespa, gave its saddle a pat, and left it to rest on a strip of dry grass between the beach and the road. He walked down to the water and splashed his dusty face and hair. He felt like eating something, but fatigue won out over hunger. He lay down on the warm sand and fell asleep.

The next morning, he was awakened by the musky breath of a dog with a dirty reddish coat. He had never before seen the sun rise out of the sea, inundating the water with a dazzling red light. He drank in the view with greedy eyes, and observed to the strange dog: "The sea is beautiful! Life is beautiful!" Then he set off again, the dog loping along behind him,

becoming progressively—hare—rabbit—mouse—fly—gnat—
and finally nothing but asphalt in the Vespa's rearview mirror.

It happened on the Sibari Plain, just a few hours later.
Giorgio Bellusci had turned off into the countryside, far from
the paved road. He had lowered himself into a comfortable
position behind a shrub, and now he was relieving himself in
blessed peace, thinking about Roccalba. He was leaving
behind him a life of boredom and a family that, in his way, he
loved, no question about that, but a family that didn't understand him, who dismissed his dream of rebuilding the Fondaco
del Fico as a youthful obsession he would forget as soon as he
was married and had a wife and children to think of. Just then,
the Vespa roared to life at the first kick-start, shattering the
silence. He leapt to his feet and ran along behind the bush
toward the mule track. He was a fool, true. But who would
have thought it? There wasn't a soul for miles, only swallows
flying overhead and crickets singing in the trees. Sons of bitches. There were two of them, and he saw them roar off at high
speed, on his Vespa, with his food, and all the flagons, and the
money that he had hidden in the hollow underside of the
scooter's saddle, too. Now here he was, panting as he struggled
through the dusty uncomfortable heat, on foot, swearing a
blue streak. If only he had them here, within reach, those low-
down thieves, he'd take care of them—a swift hard kick to the
balls. Sons of bitches. Panting.

Damp heat and dust, hills covered with wild olive trees and
prickly pears, sheep and shepherds, and every so often, luckily, a rivulet of water trickling along a broad dry riverbed,
quenching his thirst and cooling him off before it vanished
among the flat river rock and oleander bushes. He panted as
he walked and, whenever the road opened onto a crossroads,
he stopped, dazed, with no idea which direction to take, until

a shepherd or a passing peasant pointed the way. At this rate, it might well take him a month or two to reach Bari. Or he might never get there at all; he hadn't eaten a proper slice of bread and prosciutto in two days and the figs that he stole from the trees along the road filled his stomach for a couple of hours, only to empty it again with noisy gushing jets of green-ish liquid.

That journey couldn't have started any worse. Anyone else would have hightailed it for home, especially because every ten steps a wave of longing for tagliatelle with a spicy sausage sauce would flood his thoughts. But when he thought of the ribbing his friends would give him, he preferred to placate his ravenous hunger with figs and continue to follow his legs, numb with fatigue, as they lurched from one side to the other, uncertainly.

The first night, he slept beneath a wild olive tree; the leaves were lit up as brightly as a light bulb by the full moon that bathed the entire countryside in its August light. The spear grass was softer than the corn-leaf mattress he slept on back home; more important, it didn't crackle and rustle with every movement of his body. He was falling asleep, and he was amazed at how untroubled he felt, despite everything—his stomach felt fine, his head was light. "I'm going to see Patrizia," he said to himself, his eyes half open as he looked up at the brightly lit wild olive tree. Then he smiled and dropped off to sleep.

At dawn, the wild olive tree lit up with red sunlight. And at his side, as if it had watched over him through the night, was the stray dog with the dirty reddish coat. Giorgio Bellusci stretched out lazily on his spear-grass mattress as if it were Sunday morning and said to himself that, right then, he felt real good, he lacked for nothing, he missed no one, neither his parents nor his friends back in Roccalba. He stroked the dog's slobbery muzzle. The only thing he missed was the Fondaco del Fico. And Patrizia, but only for a short while longer.

He got to his feet, dusted off his trousers and shirt, and set off once again on his journey. The dog followed him, stubbornly. "Yah, yah, go on, git!" Giorgio Bellusci yelled at him, but the dog's only response was an affectionate whine. So, since it seemed they would be traveling together, he decided to give the dog a name that had been buzzing around his head since he was a child: Milord.

Oppressive heat and dust, and here and there a solitary fig tree, the fruit increasingly sere and withered, ready to come back to spiteful life in his belly, while Milord, even hungrier than he was, hunted lizards and field mice, like a cat. The days passed, and Giorgio Bellusci began to regret ever leaving. Sheep and shepherds had vanished; paved roads and steeples of bell towers were gone as well. A man like him, Giorgio Bellusci reflected, someone who couldn't even find the way to Bari, would never lay eyes on Patrizia. He was wandering the countryside aimlessly, noticed only by the numerous swifts that flew close overhead, whizzing high into the muggy sky only to come hurtling back as if by ricochet, black projectiles that grazed his hair, splattering one of his shoulders with droppings. And yet, not even in those moments of complete bewilderment did he feel any longing for Roccalba, his parents, or his friends. In fact, he thought of them with annoyance, and he was equally annoyed when he thought of Bari, a place he might never see: all things considered, that would be no tragedy, or maybe it would, certainly it would, because—Giorgio Bellusci thought to himself—if you tell everyone, I'm going to Bari, and then you wind up lost in the countryside like a little child, then you're really just a nobody, and you thought you were somebody, someone special, smarter than most of the others, because it was clear to you that it's pure stupidity to die as you were born, a jackass that never became a horse, a tree placidly rooted where it stands for a lifetime. Here was the tragedy—a brutal awakening in the wide-open countryside after having savored the first few moments of a sweet dream. Poor Giorgio, I hardly recognize you anymore. Then, in a burst of furious pride, Giorgio Bellusci closed both eyes tight and began running. Either I slam into a tree or I find the right way, he said to himself, aware that it was a crazy idea. But he stuck to it: he never opened his eyes, and continued running, with Milord chasing after him, barking happily, and the swifts shrilled overhead, making a hellish din. Go, Giorgio, go! Run, run, run! Now and again he'd catch his foot in the treacherous roots of a strawberry-tree or a downy oak, or maybe a tamarisk or a moss rose, or heather, or who knows what, or he'd stumble over Milord who was always underfoot; but he never fell. It was something he knew how to do—when he was a boy he used to scamper—eyes screwed tight—down the narrow lanes that ran from his neighborhood to the main square. Only once had he slammed into the soft belly of a tall, fat man. His father, who had cried with real concern: "Where the hell are you running with your eyes shut?" As he started off again at a dead run, he called back: "To the piazza, pop; can't you see?"

He had been running straight ahead for about ten minutes, without encountering any insurmountable obstacles when, at the top of a short uphill stretch, he heard a car horn, Milord barking, and, a second later, a screech of brakes that made him open his eyes wide.

Right in front of him, in a cloud of dust, a red automobile shaped like a turtle stood huffing and chuffing, with a bald man at the wheel—pale, angry, and swearing furiously in a foreign language.

Once the man cooled down and even offered, in clumsy Italian, to give him a ride, gesturing for the dog to get in as well, Giorgio Bellusci learned that his name was Hans

Heumann. He was German and twenty-five years old, though, being bald, he looked much older. With a mixture of words and gestures, the two men explained their respective destinations: the German was heading south, into Calabria, and not for tourism, but for work; he was an aspiring photographer; Giorgio Bellusci was traveling north, to Bari, and not for tourism, but for . . . "Well, just because, for no good reason," his voice trailed off, his chapped lips barely moving. Hans Heumann understood that the young man was exhausted and hungry as a wolf, so he offered to treat him to a meal in the first trattoria they chanced upon.

During their lunch, while Giorgio Bellusci stuffed himself with pasta and spicy tripe, gulping down a heavy wine that tasted like fruit juice and tossing chunks of meat to Milord, carelessly belching with smiling eyes, Hans Heumann asked him if he'd like to be his guide in Calabria; he could rest up, sleep in a hotel bed, eat in a trattoria, all expenses paid, of course. Maybe Giorgio Bellusci hadn't understood: he kept eating, belching, and said nothing. Then Hans Heumann added that he would be glad to accompany him to Bari, too. Take it or leave it. At that point, Giorgio Bellusci said, sure, certainly, yes definitely, thank you, and suddenly stopped belching.

And so, the two men and the dog Milord traveled from one end of Calabria to the other. While Hans Heumann snapped photographs of peasants coming back from the countryside wrapped in heavy black capes like bandits, flocks of sheep enveloped in blinding sunlight, women sitting in rows on low walls in front of their homes or sliding dough into ovens to be baked into bread, barefoot children with the faces of adults, Giorgio Bellusci saw places like nothing he had ever seen: villages perched only inches from dizzying abysses, the marker atop the Aspromonte where Garibaldi had been wounded in battle, a castle surrounded by the waters of the sea, a solitary marble column, mountains studded with Loricate pines and, enjoying pride of place among them, the oldest tree of its kind in Europe, which had long ago turned one thousand years old. The bald man, Hans the German, had only been looking for company, and certainly needed no guide. He was better educated than Giorgio and all of Roccalba put together, and then some! And if there were something that Hans didn't know, he would just look it up in a book entitled *Old Calabria*, written by an English traveler in the early years of the twentieth century. Hans Heumann was not merely well educated; he was observant, and nothing escaped his notice. The camera that he carried on a strap around his neck was like a third eye, perhaps even more acute than the other two, ready to reach out and freeze an instant of life. And he was, of course, a man of his word. When the first rains began to fall, in late September, he decided to head back north to Hamburg, but first he drove Giorgio Bellusci to Bari to see Patrizia, as promised, and afterward to Roccalba, Milord riding along the whole way.

They stopped at the Fondaco del Fico along the way, and Giorgio Bellusci fondly walked over to the stone wall with scorch marks at the top. Then he told the story of three travelers and a dog named Milord who arrived at the Fondaco del Fico one October day in 1835. That was one of two things that Hans Heumann understood. The other phrase was a waking dream, and Giorgio Bellusci pronounced the words slowly, as if reciting a prayer or a devout, unassailable wish: "I want to rebuild the Fondaco del Fico, just as it was in the good old days, when my great-grandfather was alive—no, even better."

At that moment, Hans Heumann took one of the most intense photographs of his life, and Giorgio Bellusci, just as he finished making his wish, saw a brilliant light flash before his eyes, like a shooting star. And then they drove up to the village. It was the tenth of October, 1950, when—an unprecedented event!—a red Volkswagen Beetle, with a bald young man at the wheel, entered Roccalba. Giorgio Bellusci had put on weight, at least four kilos; he was stroking a dog with a gleaming reddish coat, and he smiled at everyone he met, tanned and longhaired, like some spectacularly handsome savage.

Many years later, when the dream had finally become building plans drawn up by the best engineer for miles around, and construction was about to begin, something happened that shattered the dream into shards as if it were a brittle earthenware vase. One particularly hot and muggy summer, Giorgio Bellusci was arrested.

I didn't even notice. I continued kicking a ball around, all alone, in the courtyard, and I didn't see—or I refused to see—the carabiniere van that pulled away, tires screeching, with Giorgio Bellusci sitting in back. As for the voices from the piazza that the fiery breeze carried echoing through the alleyways, emptied for the noontime meal, they seemed no shriller, no more excited than usual.

I had arrived in Roccalba just a few days before, and I still felt stunned by that summer, swollen with dusty humid heat, that had descended over me the instant I climbed out of my father's Volvo, and that still held me in its grip.

I was eager to go to the beach. There it was, only a few miles away, just waiting to cool me down, but my parents were taking their time. They were constantly wandering around the streets and lanes of Roccalba, sticky with sweat, smiling, kissing anyone who came within reach: toothless old women, young men in shorts, girls in miniskirts, elderly men with mourning buttons on their shirts. I would cover my face with my arm and, if there was no alternative, I would let the girls kiss me. Of course, I could guess the reasons for my mother's euphoria—after all, she was coming home to her birthplace after a year away—but what baffled me was Klaus's laughter; when he was tired, the laugh changed to a fixed smile, as if he were about to have his picture taken. What did he have to laugh and smile about? He was usually moody or depressed or preoccupied; he knew ten words of Italian; and he couldn't understand a word of the strange dialect that they speak in Roccalba.

We'd come back home for lunch and dinner.

My grandmother would hug me tight to her big firm belly and then she'd uncover all the pots and pans, giving me a special preview of the delicacies that she'd prepared: stuffed eggplant, spicy sautéed peppers, fava beans or chickpeas cooked in an earthenware pot, homemade pasta or lasagna, smothered with lamb or goat-meat sauces, anise-flavored ricotta ravioli of the Sila. And then there were her specialties: mussels with potatoes and zucchini, squash-blossom fritters, and orecchiette with turnip greens, all recipes that she had brought with her from Puglia. My grandmother would smile as she watched me, my mouth watering, and I would throw my arms around her neck and kiss her in gratitude. She was a short woman, like my mother, with a large soft bosom that drooped down onto her belly, forming a pair of lovely camel humps. My grandmother had no sharp edges, and that was why I liked her best of all. Also, she was one of those few women who reached old age with her own teeth, clean and white. She spent all day in her house, which she kept orderly and clean as a whistle, just like a house in a commercial; she was courteous but a little distant with the women in the neighborhood, almost as if she wanted it to be clear that she had very little in common with them, since she came from a big city, Bari, and a wealthy family in the olive-oil business.

Giorgio Bellusci always came in when we were already seated at the table. I could never bring myself to call him Grandpa, try as I might. Nor could I call him by name, as my father sometimes did. I never called him anything; it hurt him, though he never let it show. He was almost as tall as my father, but much more muscular, because he worked as a butcher and, in his free time, as a farmer. He owned a flock of sheep and a herd of calves, as well; two of the village's sheepherders looked after them. He sold fresh milk, ricotta, *provola,* and seasoned cheeses; he slaughtered the fattened animals himself, after stunning them with a fist to the forehead. Everyone said that he was a prodigious worker and, as I noticed myself, a prodigious talker. He would talk nonstop about the hundreds of things that he had done that day, and the hundreds of things that remained to be done, especially the work on the Fondaco del Fico, the ruins of the old inn just outside town that he dreamed of turning into a little hotel and restaurant. He talked in a loud voice, as if he were addressing the entire village of Roccalba. Everyone else would nod silently; my father smiled without knowing why he was smiling; sometimes my mother would ask questions about the future Fondaco del Fico, and offer advice without being asked—for instance, she recommended building a pool for the hotel. She, too, talked at the top of her lungs. Yes, I was stunned by the relentless heat, but also by the sheer volume of those frantic voices. I felt as if I had wandered into a village full of deaf people.

Giorgio Bellusci was unfailingly cheerful, at the outset. First, because the family was back together again. Second, because business was going well—even too well, he said—especially in the summer, when the village doubled in population because the emigrants would come back home from the north, and he sold three times the meat because the emigrants didn't pay attention to how much they spent during the holidays: they devoured meat, God bless them, to prove that they had plenty of money.

Then, beginning on the first Sunday in July, Giorgio Bellusci's mood darkened. He kept talking, but it was clear that he was bitter and, in the most convulsive moments, gleams of sheer hatred blazed from his shiny brown eyes, streaked here and there with black like a pair of luminous chestnuts.

I managed to piece together the details of what was happening to him years later with the help of my mother; I was surprised to remember things that I had canceled from my memory almost as soon as they happened.

Everything began, then, in the late morning of that first Sunday in July. The butcher shop was empty, and Giorgio Bellusci was putting the unsold meat back into the walk-in cooler. He did this work with a calculated sluggishness, lingering longer than necessary in front of the open cooler door. Outside, the malevolent muggy heat was bearing down cruelly, and the gusts of cool air refreshed his sweaty head and long bare arms, spattered here and there with calf's blood.

A powerful car came to a stop in front of the butcher shop. Two men sat inside. The driver remained behind the wheel. The passenger, a well-dressed young man, got out, looked around, and panted in the intense heat. He stepped into the butcher shop and uttered a courteous greeting in an Italian that had a strong Calabrian accent: "Good morning, chief. How are things?" He was wearing a light-blue linen suit, with patches of sweat under the armpits.

"Good morning to you, sir," Giorgio Bellusci replied. "You're just in time, I was just closing up. I still have some rump left over; around here they don't understand quality meat; they just look at the price. This meat melts in your mouth. We raise our own calves."

The man touched the rump roast with a finger, as if to see if it were really tender. He smiled, as if pleased. He said: "Business is good, right, chief?"

Giorgio Bellusci replied: "I can't complain, thanks."

"And the land out of town? And the livestock? I hear you're planning to buy some vineyards down by the river. And this brilliant plan of yours to build a hotel! The Fondaco del Fico! A stroke of genius! My grandfather told me it was once a first-class inn, back in the day. Everyone stopped there, all the travelers. You know, we need a place like that here. The closest hotel is down at the beach. You'll make loads of money, in the summer at least. So you're expanding! Getting ahead. It looks like you're a guy with a future."

Giorgio Bellusci drew a deep breath of cool air from the refrigerator that he had opened again, and glanced suspiciously at the man: "Where do you come from, that you know so much about me? You know more than my wife does."

For the first time, the man looked at him with an arrogant expression.

"I come from where my mother made me. That shouldn't be any of your business. You need to keep your mind on getting ahead, that's what we like to see. You'll have our blessing; you'll have our protection. You'll pay a small percentage, on the last Sunday of every month. I'll stop by to pick up our cut personally. You won't have to worry about a thing. You're in good hands."

Giorgio Bellusci couldn't believe his ears; he didn't want to believe it. He was so surprised that he didn't know how to respond: whether he should smack him in the mouth with the heavy rump roast or just laugh in his face. He tried replying ironically: "Huh? I think you've got me mixed up with someone who's won the lottery. I earn my living with these." And he held up his big calloused hands.

"Don't try to be funny, we know all about you, right down to how many hairs you have in your asshole. Pay up, and don't be a stubborn asshole. Or you'll wind up being sorry," he said with an aggressive tone, pressing his finger against Giorgio Bellusci's blood-smeared smock.

Giorgio Bellusci picked up the old razor-sharp knife that he used to quarter sides of veal, and laid it on the stranger's finger. "Get that finger off me, or I'll slice it clean off," he said, his eyes bulging out as he spoke. "I'll cut you into little pieces and toss you to my herd dogs."

Instinctively, the man pulled his finger back. He moved back a step and slipped one hand under his jacket. Then he changed his mind. He said: "We'll see you next Sunday, hard man. A little bird tells me you'll change your mind—word of honor!" He walked quickly out of the shop, got into the car, and was gone.

That same night, someone set fire to the door of the butcher shop.

The following morning, surrounded by a curious, incredulous crowd, Giorgio Bellusci loudly said: "It was an old door, anyway!" Before nightfall, he'd had a shiny new aluminum door fitted. "That won't be so easy to burn." He couldn't help grinning. And not another word on the matter.

At home, he chattered loudly and said—speaking to my mother—that the idea of the pool wasn't a bad one at that, and that he would talk to his engineer about it. Then he proposed a toast—"To the new door!"—and drank deeply from his glass of ice-cold wine. A moment later he fell silent; he kept on drinking as he stared out the open window at nothing in particular.

That evening, Aunt Elsa, Uncle Bruno, and their daughter, Teresa, ate dinner with us. They lived on the third story of my grandparents' big house, and they had just come back from the beach. They didn't feel like talking either, though they were usually such chatterboxes.

My mother tried to lift her father's spirits, in the only way possible: harking back to the happy times when the Fondaco del Fico was the most famous inn in all of Calabria, or at least the one most frequently mentioned by foreign travelers of bygone centuries. She, good schoolteacher that she was, knew all the names of those travelers by heart, and she would serve them up at every opportunity, even in Hamburg, especially if we had German guests at our home. Even I could tell, when I was only a child, that she was trying to astonish her listeners, in the way she pronounced those names, launching each one from her heart-shaped lips like a kiss: Swin-bur-ne, de Ta-vel, Vi-vant De-non, Stol-berg, Ga-lan-ti, Kep-pel Craven, Tom-ma-si-ni, Le-nor-mant, Di-dier, and Diù-mà (as she sounded it out in Italian)—Alexandre Dumas, author of *The Three Musketeers*. Our guests would listen politely, but it was clear that they didn't believe her, any more than my father believed her stories—and, to make matters worse, he didn't even care. So my mother would make everyone look at her university thesis on Stolberg, a German traveler who had stayed at the Fondaco del Fico at the end of the eighteenth century; she had a degree, she taught Italian in a school in Hamburg; she, Rosanna Bellusci, was an expert on the subject. She had read every book that mentioned the Fondaco del Fico. If they chose not to believe her, and, in particular, if that "certified turd," her husband, Klaus, who had been a troublemaker from birth, chose not to believe her, then my mother would produce her second piece of documentation—incontestable: a book by Vito Teti entitled *Il Fondaco del Fico*, a Bible to her, which usually persuaded the most skeptical guests, but still left my father entirely indifferent.

That evening my mother revealed that according to an English traveler writing in the late eighteenth century, the Fondaco del Fico was the inn from which Cicero himself wrote a series of letters to a certain Atticus. An error in transcription by a scribe had changed the Latin *Ficae* into *Sicae*, but according to the English traveler this was the place that Cicero described. My mother was just as certain about it as the Englishman was, and even though no one present was familiar with any of the names mentioned, the news served to enhance the aura of respect that surrounded the Fondaco del Fico. Even Uncle Bruno, an unrepentant devil's advocate who never missed an opportunity to contradict my mother, nodded in agreement. My father nodded and smiled the whole time, too, but he may not have even understood the topic of conversation.

Giorgio Bellusci drank another gulp of cold wine, wiped his lips with the back of his hand, and said, "Sure, all this is important, it enhances the lineage of our Fondaco del Fico, it brings it fame and respect. But to me, it's about something more! I couldn't say what, just something more!" And as he spoke, he looked directly at me, his breath driving the words into my eyes, along with the smell of wine.

I was beginning to be bored. From the balcony in my room, I could see the waves of the sea in the distance, hidden by a veil of shimmering muggy heat; playing hide and seek (or "*giocare all'ammuccia*," as they say in Roccalba) with the neighborhood kids only tired me out, making me sweat like a bear.

For two days in a row my folks went into town with Giorgio Bellusci, to see his engineer. They got back to Roccalba at dinnertime. And so, no beach. On the other hand, Giorgio Bellusci had regained his cheerful calm; he even ignored the whirlwind of rumors about the fire, that is, the reasons for and the consequences of the fire; subjects that the people of the village never tired of guessing at, theorizing about, and asserting with confidence. Giorgio Bellusci was dismissive about his fellow villagers: "Everyone in this village is a soccer coach or a police detective. But, most of all, they're meddlers who won't mind their own business, on pure principle." And backbiters, of course. In fact, someone went so far as to say that Giorgio Bellusci had set fire to his own door, just to pocket the insurance money.

The villagers were obliged to retract that last slur soon enough. Some peasants who happened to be passing through the countryside near the Fondaco del Fico noticed that a hundred or so grape vines and at least forty olive trees had been cut down. Three of them hurried over to my grandparents' house, one after another, each with cap or hat in hand, as if in mourning for the dead plants.

"They cut them down last night, you can tell," they said. "Because with the heat of the sun today, the leaves of the vines withered like peppers fried in oil, and the grapes look like they were slow roasted. Only the olives remained unchanged, shiny and small, unusable. Years of work ruined without pity."

Giorgio Bellusci gave each of them something to drink and did his best to conceal his rage with words that surprised the peasants: "That's fine; it means less work for me." And he even smiled, thanking them for the information.

Afterward, he went into the countryside alone, to see with his own eyes and to touch with his own hands the dead trees and vines. Upon his return, he said nothing; when his family asked him worried questions, he answered: "Come on, let's eat instead." But during dinner he slipped into a bad mood, and it rubbed off on everyone else. It felt like one of the wakes that they hold after a funeral in Hamburg. Worse. Even my father stopped smiling.

Then Giorgio Bellusci invited us outside, onto the balcony. First he brought us something to drink, orangeade for Teresa and me, wine and ice-cold limoncello for the grownups. Then he began to look us at in a strange, almost mocking way, or maybe it just seemed that way to me because of the pale evening light that illuminated his face fitfully. Suddenly I noticed—everyone noticed—that his gaze was catching fire, returning to life, becoming thuggish. And since no one had had the strength or the courage to raise his morale, he did it by himself and consoled the others, too.

"I want to give you some good news," he said, his face turned toward the Fondaco del Fico, invisible in the darkness enveloping the countryside—though his burning eyes could certainly see it. "Wait just a minute," he added. He walked into the living room and from there to the master bedroom. He came back a few minutes later. He was holding an inlaid wooden box in his hands. We all waited anxiously to hear the good news. But first Giorgio Bellusci told us a story.

The three travelers, with a dog named Milord, arrive at the Fondaco del Fico around noon. They're covered in dust from head to foot; they look like ghosts with bright eyes, outsiders. One of them has the mischievous face of a young local; the other two are certainly foreigners, perhaps Englishmen. Expensive Damascus steel double-barreled shotguns are slung over their shoulders. The innkeeper, Gioacchino Bellusci, has no doubts, even though he has not yet heard them say a word. He's already looked them up and down, half mistrustfully, half ceremoniously, evaluating them with an expert eye; they wouldn't be spending the night, they are looking around them too hastily for that. They'll be asking for something to eat for themselves and some feed for their mounts. Sure enough. They ask for a little food for Milord as well, and they tie him up in the stables, next to the mules. The young mule driver does the talking for the trio. He comes from Pizzo, he says. The other two are French, one a painter, the other a writer. Two gentlemen. They're headed for Cosenza.

The innkeeper Gioacchino Bellusci yells to his wife to prepare some macaroni with chickpeas—mouthwatering, he assures them—but the French writer pulls two fistfuls of chestnuts out of his pockets. He courteously asks if the innkeeper could see to roasting them under the embers. He's not hungry, he claims; in reality, he just doesn't like macaroni; he finds it repugnant. He is a man about thirty, with a careful, slightly restless gaze, with a round glowing face, like a full moon. His name is Alexandre Dumas, and, while awaiting his lunch, he begins writing rapidly in a sort of book that he pulls out of his haversack; the other Frenchman pulls out a stick of charcoal and skillfully begins sketching a portrait of the Bellusci family: the stout figure of the innkeeper preparing to pour out the fine wine that they will drink with their meal; standing next to him, his son, with glittering, slightly wild eyes, and, in the background, the daughter, leaning on her mother's flounce skirt.

Gioacchino Bellusci gladly lets the artist sketch him; the request does not catch him off guard. Many odd travelers come through the Fondaco del Fico—foreigners, Sicilians, Neapolitans, traveling along the road between the Calabrias or between the two seas, and they stop at the inn like bees setting down inside a flower. They can't help but stop there. And they would stop there back when his father was still alive, bless his soul, and before that, as well, they had always stopped. Not just travelers, whether for business or pleasure, but soldiers on the march, too, as often as not. The ancestor who selected that lovely spot to build an inn hundreds of years before had been a man with an eye for the main chance, a farsighted man indeed. And so it is. When travelers reach the Fondaco del Fico, whether from north or south, from the Ionian or the Tyrrhenian, they are always tired and hungry, as are Alexandre Dumas and his friend, who in the meantime has finished his sketch and, at the insistence of the Bellusci family, has even made a gift of it—he, so protective of his work—and in exchange he takes nothing more than a bottle of wine.

Before settling down to their meal, the strangers set book and sketch on a clean, bare table. When they set off again—after little more than two hours in the inn—Dumas's book is left behind, beneath the sketch, signed Jadin.

And in the end, despite the earthquake and two floods that had unleashed their fury on the Fondaco del Fico, despite the roaring fire that nearly destroyed the entire inn, that odd charcoal sketch and that book with its brown leather cover had been handed down, intact, to him, Giorgio Bellusci, as if by some miracle. Now he kept them inside an inlaid wooden box, locked in a dresser drawer, like holy relics. He never let anyone touch them, fearful that by taking them out they might be damaged or even—old as they were—crumble to bits. At the very most, he would let others smell them. In fact, that evening too, he opened the box carefully and then, gripping it tight in both hands, he wafted it beneath the noses of everyone in his family.

When my turn came, I stretched my neck out as far as I could. I just glimpsed the sketch by Jadin and, beneath it, two rectangular strips of Dumas's dark-brown cover, as a whiff of bergamot rose, surprisingly, into my nostrils.

In this same box, Giorgio Bellusci had also kept the dream of a lifetime, and that evening he finally pulled it out and proudly displayed it: "The plans have been approved. Work begins on July 26, in exactly ten days and nine hours. By this time next year, if God wishes, we'll have the finest hotel for miles around: the new Fondaco del Fico."

That was the good news.

There was a burst of spontaneous applause from Aunt Elsa, and a moment later we were all clapping for Giorgio Bellusci, who responded with little nods and a smile of genuine warmth that I had never seen before.

"Well, then we should drink a toast," said Uncle Bruno. And we all drank a toast, holding our glasses out toward the Fondaco del Fico. That evening, I believe no one gave a thought to the burnt door or the unfortunate slashed vines and felled olive trees. Instead, we were thinking of the future.

But then, Saturday morning, Giorgio Bellusci's stockmen found ten sheep and two herd dogs dead, their throats cut and their bodies hung up on hooks on the wire pasture fence, in a row, fleece bloodied, eyes staring at the sky.

Giorgio Bellusci said not a word. He stood there in silence, taking in the scene, while the herders cursed and swore, their maledictions rolling along in the ravines and echoing through the open countryside, startling the swallows in flight.

Two hours later, the ten sheep were hanging on display in the butcher shop, already quartered and available for purchase, retail, with an attractive discount.

All of Roccalba poured into the butcher shop, in a gesture of solidarity, to learn more about what had happened, as well as to buy meat at discount prices. Giorgio Bellusci talked about the quality of the meat he was selling; with his razor sharp cleaver he shaved off thin slices, hefty chops, and lungs; as usual he reeled off risqué jokes, and paid gallant compliments to all the female customers, young and old, fat and thin; he gulped down mouthfuls of chilly air from the cooler, and in response to specific questions he provided brief but courteous answers: "I don't know who it was. Yes, certainly criminals. I don't think so. No, I haven't reported it to the police. Yes, there are criminals everywhere. The world isn't like it used to be. I hope so. I don't know. No." And he looked at my father with an expression of regret, as if to apologize for what had happened. He had always told him that Roccalba was the quietest little town on earth.

By evening, only three sheep remained unsold. Giorgio Bellusci ran them into the walk-in cooler, with all the meat hooks, then he stood there, allowing his sweaty face to cool for a minute. Then, eyes wide open, he reviewed mentally the scene of the animals hanging on the fence and he slammed the cooler door shut, finally unleashing the shout that had been building up in his throat: "Sons of bitches!"

He brought home an enormous watermelon, the biggest one I had ever seen. It was cold from the walk-in cooler, and it split open the instant that Giorgio Bellusci placed the tip of a kitchen knife on the rind. Then he cut big slices for everyone; "This one is for Florian," he said, and he gave me what was known as the rooster's crest, the heart of the watermelon, so big that that night I had to get up several times to pee.

Late the following morning, Giorgio Bellusci was arrested; two hours later I was finally at the beach, a guest of one of my mother's female cousins. They were absolutely determined to keep me from learning what had happened. They wanted to spare me the shock. I was so hungry to dive into the waves, swim in the sea, and breathe salt air, that the fact that I had been sent to the beach, moreover without my parents, aroused not the slightest suspicion in my blithe state; if anything, it struck me as proper compensation for too many days spent suffocating in the muggy heat for no good reason. If my folks wanted to keep on suffering like the damned in hell, *bitte*, they could be my guests, no problem; I was more than willing to let them have my daily ration of oppressive heat. My mother's cousin was a nice woman; she had two boys—not much older but definitely more daring than me, in the water and out. Fun was assured. All the same, I have to admit that I missed my family a bit, especially in the evening, and especially my mother.

I came back to Roccalba a week later, with a tan, and found my family with faces the pale green of vomit. When I noticed that Giorgio Bellusci wasn't at dinner and asked where he had gone, my mother told me a lie. "He left for work, in northern Italy. He'll send lots of nice money down to Grandma."

"What? He has his work here in Roccalba. Why did he leave?" I might have been a child, but I wasn't an idiot.

"The money is better up north," my mother cut me off. Then with one hand she pretended to push an imaginary lock of hair off her forehead, and she covered her glistening eyes; then my grandmother went into the kitchen, where she started to blow her nose loudly.

It had been the most disastrous vacation I could remember. And as if that weren't enough, when we got back to Hamburg, my mother told me that she was pregnant. Perhaps she hoped that I would be overjoyed. She and my father certainly were. They had wanted another child for years; for me, they said, to keep me from growing up alone, the way Klaus had, an only child sick with loneliness. I said: "Oh, really?" with a great show of indifference, and turned on the television. It hurt her feelings. She muttered something unintelligible that issued from her heart-shaped lips with a trail of snail slime. I didn't care, it had hurt my feelings too. I had hoped to be spared the misfortune of having a little snot-nosed brother or sister underfoot.

My mother lived through the pregnancy in terror of shattering the porcelain doll that she carried in her belly. She sat on the sofa all day, swollen and almost motionless, reading magazines about giving birth and newborn babies. She even invited my grandmother to come up from Roccalba, the only one on earth who would gladly—and free of charge—work as a cleaning woman, cook, nanny for me, and silent audience to my mother's incessant complaints: she had pains all over and was constantly on the verge of going into labor.

My grandmother's presence in our home was a relief for everyone. Klaus, in particular, turned into a happy man, even before becoming a father for the second time, relaxed and even cheerful thanks to his saint of a mother-in-law, who kept his house clean, cared for his son and his wife, and cooked like an angel. He'd come home from the bank where he worked as a director for public relations, eat a leisurely dinner, and then—instead of shutting himself up in his study to write pamphlets and articles that were incomprehensible to me, even the head-lines—he would play with me or kid around with Grandma; he was always sweet with my mother, and, in moments of special tenderness, he would lay his bald head on her big belly that grew from day to day. Never before had he spent so much time with us.

My grandmother never left the house unless it was to go grocery shopping with me. It was fun to go to the supermarket with her. She would select fruit and vegetables with her own hands, even though it was forbidden to touch the produce in a German supermarket, and sometimes she even tried to bargain on the prices. Then, home, to cook. She was never still, not even for an instant, constantly in motion, practically at a dead run, up and down the stairs, keeping our little two-story house clean. Plump as she was, you'd have expected her to sweat, get tired or out of breath. But she never did. Her two lovely camel humps bounced up and down lightly and gracefully on her chest. At night, before going to sleep, she would tell me stories about her own family; true stories, she insisted, like the story about one of her great-grandfathers, an officer in the army, who fell in love with a princess who was already married, and was later killed in a duel. She never talked to me about Giorgio Bellusci. If, by mischance, any of us—or even she—happened to mention his name, her eyes immediately filled with tears. Though I was only a child, I understood that she really loved Giorgio Bellusci; that she was crying because he had left her to go live who knew where.

I had no doubts about it: when I grew up, I planned to marry a woman who was like Grandma in every way. My future wife, however, would have heart-shaped lips, like my mother.

*

On March 23, Marco, my baby brother, was born. All of the resentment that had smoldered inside me when he was kicking in my mother's belly was transformed into a tender glow of love as soon as they put him in my arms, at the hospital. He was a half-ugly little fat thing, with puffy eyes and sparse blond hair, like a wet baby chick, as he lay placidly suckling at my mother's breast; her bosom had become enormous ever since her fat belly went down, with erect nipples that sprayed milk as soon as Marco touched them with his chubby little fingers. Everyone said that Marco looked like me, but I didn't think I was so ugly.

In the weeks that followed, I was forced to eat my words. Not only did he resemble me, but I could no longer deny that he was a beautiful baby: he already smiled at me, he already recognized me, maybe he already loved me.

These were untroubled days: my grandmother was still living with us; my father would dandle his baby in his arms when he came home from the bank, and compete with me to see who could make Marco laugh harder; my mother was slender and relaxed again, and she was getting ready to return to her work as an Italian teacher. And, most important, she had begun to talk about the Fondaco del Fico again, as if it were a distant relative, whom she missed.

It was during that same period that, without warning, one evening, Hans Heumann, Klaus's father, came to see us, with a young redheaded babe, wearing flashy makeup.

"Allow me to introduce my wife, Hélène. She's from Paris," said Hans Heumann, and I felt my face flush in embarrassment, because I had assumed she was his daughter. If it had been hard for me to call Giorgio Bellusci Grandpa, just imagine how hard it was with Hans Heumann.

He would come to see us once every two or three years, and so I had a hard time even remembering what he looked like. In fact, it had taken one of my teachers to tell me that he was a world-renowned photographer: "Is it true that you are the grandson of Hans Heumann, the famous photographer?" I didn't know how to answer her. He lived all over, first in New York, then in Tokyo, and then in Paris, and he never sent letters or called us on the phone.

Klaus didn't like talking about his father, except when my mother would prod him into doing so when dining with friends. She liked to boast about her famous father-in-law, though lately she couldn't stand him.

That evening, I liked Hans Heumann a lot. He was dressed simply, in a pair of blue jeans and a dark-brown leather jacket, and he looked like Klaus's older brother, not his father. He kept one arm wrapped around his young wife the whole time, as if he were afraid she might run away. He was bald, like my father, but he had the small, light-blue eyes of a young boy, surrounded by a spider's web of fine wrinkles. With his little eyes, first he examined Marco, the new arrival, and then me, in detail, like an expert pediatrician: hair and forehead, eyes and ears, nose and mouth, hands and arms were all observed carefully, and if possible, stroked with his free hand. With his other hand, Hans was caressing Hélène.

My father stayed in a corner, embarrassed and red to the top of his shiny head. I couldn't figure out why he was behaving that way. He seemed like an awkward schoolboy before his teacher, not a son in front of his father. I broke away from Hans Heumann's caressing hand and went over to curl up on my father's knees, and he gave me a grateful kiss on the forehead.

When my grandmother emerged from the kitchen and walked into the living room, unaware of who had come to see us, Hans Heumann recognized her immediately, even though he had seen her only once before, a great many years ago, when she was a girl and as slender as my mother. Hans jumped to his feet, kissed her hand, and made a deep bow. My grandmother had recognized him too and now she repeated over and over, as if enchanted: "But how young you still look, Signor Oimànn." Grandma was clearly very pleased at that unannounced visit, perhaps happier than anyone else; her eyes shone, and the guests immediately forgave her for her heedless gaffe: "What a lovely daughter you have, Signor Oimànn, you look alike as two peas in a pod!" Then Hans asked her with his rudimentary Italian about Giorgio Bellusci, and why he wasn't there. Two big teardrops started from her eyes at once, as if he had sliced into an onion right in front of her eyes. And before Grandma began telling the story, my mother made me kiss everyone good night and took me to bed.

When I woke up, I found out that Hans and Hélène had left for Paris.

A few weeks later a postcard arrived for me from Tokyo. Hans Heumann had written me: "Dear Florian, you're a wonderful child. I love you. Give a kiss to Marco for me. Yours, Hans."

I gave Marco a kiss and that evening I showed the postcard to my father. He was astonished and, turning the card over in his hands, he said: "Well, look at that. The old man's turning soft, maybe he's changing." Then he announced: "He'll come to see us soon." But he was alone in believing it, or hoping it. Though maybe I did too, a little.

My mother answered him tersely: "You're wrong, sweetheart. He'll come back only when we have another child. That is, never."

Perhaps time would prove her right. For now, she managed to make Klaus lose his temper. Actually, to make him explode. I'd never seen him display such eye-bugging, mouth-foaming anger. "You bitch!" he shouted. "You filthy bitch. You could never stand my father because you never saw a *pfennig* of his wealth."

I hadn't understood the reasons for the fight, and I didn't understand my father's reaction. But I did understand that Hans Heumann was wealthy, I understood all the curses and dirty words that my parents heaped on each other, and I liked this unknown ferocious side to Klaus; my mother's ferocious side was already all too familiar. Unfortunately, when it looked like they were about to come to blows, my grandmother pushed me into my bedroom, and I could hear only the distant echoes of their shouting.

They didn't talk for three weeks. When he came home from the bank, Klaus shut himself up in his study, emerging only after we had all gone to bed. He would eat in the kitchen; my grandmother would set aside spaghetti with meatballs for him, and then he would go sleep in the attic.

He was the one who finally gave in, one evening when Marco had a harmless temperature. On the other hand, my mother was too hardheaded, and if he had waited for her to take the first step toward peace, they still wouldn't be talking today.

Then my grandmother announced that she would be heading back to Roccalba at the end of the month, and so both my parents joined forces to persuade her to stay: they were in total agreement, they spoke in perfect unison, they laid out a hundred reasons and excuses to convince her to stay. They told her that she was safe in Hamburg. Roccalba could still be dangerous. I had no idea what they meant. Maybe they were referring to the danger of earthquakes, which were common events around Roccalba. But Grandma was implacable, she saw no danger, she couldn't stay away from her home, the rest of her family, the countryside, she said, any longer.

I don't even know why, but I burst into tears. And that was when my grandmother gave up: "All right, I'll stay a little longer."

She stayed for another five or six months, until Marco could walk and break my toys, and say "cacca," and "Oma," and "Flo'ian." It was the end of June and my summer vacation had begun just a few days before. And so my parents, forming a common front, had the great idea (as they called it) of sending me to Roccalba with Grandma for six weeks. At the beginning of August, Klaus would drive down to get me. My mother, instead, would stay in Hamburg with Marco, afraid that her chubby little boy might melt in the buttery heat of Roccalba.

The Fondaco del Fico really was a wall charred at its jagged top, but to my child's eyes, it looked like a dinosaur's enormous cavity-ridden incisor. It stood surrounded by a tangled island of thorn bushes, tamarisks, thistles, and prickly pears all growing wild, concealing further blocks of masonry, broken roof tiles, and steps. All around it lay Giorgio Bellusci's land, a sea of grape vines and olive trees, stretching between the rocky floors of two wide riverbeds, lined with oleanders.

Grandma had insisted that I accompany my uncle and my aunt and little Teresa to pick apricots, greengage plums, and mulberries. Teresa, who hated getting dirty, sat on a big stone and panted in the heat. I, on the other hand, wandered around in the intense heat, examining the vines that had been left to grow wild, climbing trees, and stuffing myself with fruit. I studied the cavity-ridden dinosaur incisor and, moody as I was about that forced vacation, I couldn't help but dwell on poisonous thoughts. Yeah, right, a hotel set between two filthy riverbeds without any water! In the middle of the countryside! Just four miles from a village infested with flies and muggy heat! If Giorgio Bellusci hadn't vanished from that horrible place, they would have locked him up in an insane asylum. Sure, I was angry with Giorgio Bellusci more than anyone, but I was angry with my mother and Klaus, too, and their brilliant notion of sending me to Roccalba; and I was even angry with my grandmother, who had agreed to the idea enthusiastically.

Most of all, though, I was angry with myself because, to keep from disappointing her, I had said: "Sure, okay."

God, how I regretted it. Perhaps it showed, because Teresa kept looking at me with concern and asking me: "What's the matter, Florian? What did we do to you?"

Teresa was a little ten-year-old doll, a slightly chubby Barbie, with a little gang of girlfriends, all of them nicely dressed and impeccably coiffed like her, and all of them just as intolerable as she was. She would invite them over, one at a time, and I would have to put up with all their coquettish flirting and allusions, little love letters that they'd copied from who knew where, surprise kisses on the cheek when I was absorbed in a television show, and sly giggles that chased me into my bedroom, where I would slam the door behind me.

The most annoying of them all was Martina, a twelve-year-old who claimed she was my girlfriend. She would make jealous scenes and, when I didn't react, her pride offended, she would send me to the devil and rush out of the house. An hour later, though, she was back, wearing skimpy T-shirts that revealed her small, newly blossomed breasts.

Aunt Elsa would tease me: "Why, what a lot of girlfriends he has, this handsome Florian of mine!" And she'd hug me and cuddle me, as if she understood that I missed my mother terribly and that she resembled my mother more than anyone else in the family: she was petite, fine-featured, and fine-limbed, with heart-shaped lips, a long curly head of hair, a bosom barely restrained by her necklines. Her bosom was so joyful and inviting that sometimes Uncle Bruno squeezed it as if he wanted to test its heft. One afternoon I saw him on the balcony with my own eyes. My aunt was leaning against the railing and he lifted and lowered her breasts, holding them proudly in his cupped hands. I was jealous of Uncle Bruno: he could squeeze and touch Aunt Elsa whenever he wanted, in the light of the sun or the darkness of their master bedroom, where an enormous bed enjoyed pride of place, surrounded by the mirrors on the armoires. Fortunately, Aunt Elsa loved me too, and she paid me compliments that made me blush: "Why, mothers have stopped making boys this handsome, and even when they do, they've still got nothing on you. With these dark eyes and blond hair, you'll massacre the girls' hearts." But for the moment, I had to make do with those intolerable and insistent Barbie dolls buzzing in and out of our house like flies. Like lying flies. Martina was spreading a rumor that I had kissed her on the lips. In reality, it was she who had brushed her lips against mine as we were dancing during a little party that Teresa had thrown, a party at which I was the only boy.

I was only completely free of Martina and the other flies on the weekend, when my aunt and uncle took me to the beach between Copanello and Soverato. "Here," Uncle Bruno would say, as if he were reciting poetry, "the wily Ulysses met the lovely Nausicaa." The beach was practically deserted, and Uncle Bruno liked it because it was as far as possible from the Tyrrhenian beaches so popular with those pains-in-the-neck from Roccalba, he said, and from their prying eyes. Teresa, without her girlfriends, withdrew into hostile silence, distant even from me, and read magazines under the beach umbrella the whole time, to my enormous enjoyment. That way, I could admire in blessed peace the little fish swimming in the crystal-clear water or the drops of perspiration on my aunt's breasts, breasts that her swimsuit could barely contain and that my uncle's possessive hands, with the excuse of applying suntan lotion, massaged without restraint. I would swim for as long as possible, to keep from having to look at those pudgy, hairy hands. When I came back to shore, I'd throw myself down belly-first on the sand and sneak glances at my beautiful aunt as she roasted slowly in the sun without complaining, while Teresa panted impatiently and my uncle finally went in the water, not very far from dry land, because he didn't know how to swim and couldn't rely entirely on his belly, which could have kept him safely on the surface like a life jacket.

At the end of the day, as soon as we set foot back in the house, Martina and Teresa's other girlfriends resumed their pestering, and refused to leave me in peace until dinnertime. When I couldn't take it anymore, I locked myself in my grandparents' enormous bedroom, which proved to be not only invulnerable but also the coolest room in the house, with a pair of spacious French doors that gave onto a balcony that enjoyed a view of the nearby Tyrrhenian Sea. Often my grandmother would be in her bedroom, busily cleaning with damp rags the armoires, dressers, and night tables, the bed head, and—most important of all—the frames of the old black-and-white photographs. She was in those old pictures, alone, younger and prettier than Aunt Elsa, then with her chubby little daughters, and with Giorgio Bellusci, who was younger too, and lost in thought, with one arm around her shoulder and the other on her arm, as if he were leaning on her in a moment of bewilderment and dizziness. Then she would put those pictures, gleaming with youth and the damp of the rag, back exactly where they had been before: on the antique cherry-wood nine-drawer dresser looking out onto the open balcony. In one of those nine drawers—as I well remembered—was the inlaid wooden box containing Jadin's sketch and Dumas's notebook, but my grandmother wouldn't open that drawer—even under torture, she told me. "I promised your grandfather, don't ask me again, Florian, please. He'll show you. When he comes back."

"When will he come back, Grandma?"

"Soon. He'll come back soon," my grandmother replied, and she turned to stare out past the large vases overbrimming with red carnations, out to sea, doing her best to conceal the tracks of two sudden tears. Then she went back to her dusting, even though everything in the big bedroom gleamed like new, and her dusting struck me as a little crazy. I was too young to understand that in that bedroom she was dusting off her memories, keeping them shiny, caressing them lovingly. Every so often a memory would slip through her fingers and I was catapulted into an unknown world and time, following with fascination the exploits of an impertinent young man named Giorgio, who presented himself at her home one day with the long hair of a savage, accompanied by a bald foreigner named Oimànn, who had nothing to do with the two of them, and how my grandmother's father wasn't all that surprised by their sudden appearance: he had met Giorgio at Camigliatello, and he knew what kind of man he was, and fully expected that one day or another he would ask for his daughter's hand in marriage. She had been surprised, however: surprised and pleased. Sadly, her father lived scarcely long enough to see them man and wife. He had been suffering for years from an unspeakable disease, and he died just before Rosanna—my mother—was born. They could have lived in the family home in Bari, Giorgio and she; they could have lived like aristocrats. They could have gotten ahead, earned more than in Roccalba. Gotten ahead, and far more easily. Her loving father would have left them his share of the company, if they would only set up house in Bari. The olive-oil business was profitable, back then. At first, she had tried to persuade him to stay, tentatively. But Giorgio was hard as a rock on this point. Relentless. Unyielding. Obsessed. Even in his sleep, Giorgio talked about this blessed Fondaco del Fico. My grandmother sighed. Roccalba, she said, is a village of lunatics, like all villages. She put up with it only because from the balcony in her bedroom she could glimpse the sea in the distance, just like from the balcony in her father's home. At night, now that she was sleeping alone, she felt as if she could hear the voice of the sea, warm and gentle, comforting her for the grief and pain of life, the forced separations.

I would emerge from the big bedroom, proud to have been entrusted with my grandmother's bittersweet confidences, feeling at peace with myself and the world, with the muggy heat and the biting flies. But then my parents would call on the phone, and a rage would sweep over me with the shrill treachery of a swarm of wasps. I would always look for some excuse not to talk to them. Most of the time, I would lock myself in the bathroom and yell through the door that I couldn't come to the phone because I was taking a poop, or else as soon as I heard the phone ring, even if we were in the middle of a meal, I would slip away into the narrow lanes and alleys of Roccalba and stay away until it was dark.

One day, I was too slow getting away, and my grandmother plastered the receiver against my ear, forcing me to listen to Marco's affectionate little voice; he had learned to say "*Florian, komm,*" while my mother acted all stirred and touched, whispering that she missed me, and Klaus said he envied me, how nice and hot it must be, while in Hamburg it was raining. I felt like vomiting into the mouthpiece.

When I left the house to go to the piazza, I was furious at my parents—they had torn me away from Hamburg and now they were insulting my intelligence, liars and hypocrites that they were. First they cast me down into that hellish prison of humid heat, a heat that even clipped the wings of the scent of the chrysanthemums or even of armpits, that blurred the bright blue of the sea until it could no longer be seen, that swallowed up the shouts and cries of the children and the chirping voices of the old women sitting on the low walls in the narrow lanes like an invisible soundproof wall. Horrible muggy heat! And then there were the flies, the bastard flies, their intolerable buzzing, their chattering, soft and yielding like shit. I had run out of words and I had run out of patience. And the price of my awful mood was paid by a boy who had called me "Hoimammà-Potato-Eater," a nickname that the little kids of Roccalba had dreamed up for me, in a twist on my surname, Heumann. Of course, I often laughed it off when they called me that, or I would pretend for a moment to chase them; I didn't always react violently. That day, though, it was just too much. I crushed the boy to the ground with both knees, I tore at his hair with my hands, slapping his face and punching him in the nose. The little shit was bleeding, and I didn't care a bit. Drops of my sweat spattered onto his hair, face, chest; I was all sticky and I kept punching him, as if I were glued to my clothing and to the little boy whining and sobbing beneath my knees—certainly, a bit of a brat, but nowhere near as guilty as my parents and that filthy humid heat.

Suddenly, I heard a woman screaming as she rushed towards us. It was like a shot that tore through the heat and struck me in the head, leaving me even more dumbstruck than before: "You little murderer! Get off my son; you're killing him. You're a murderer like your grandfather, let him go!" And before she could get her hands on the scruff of my neck, I became a cloud of dust vanishing into the hot muggy distance.

Breathless, I stopped to rest atop a little hill just outside of the village; I flopped belly down on the dry grass. What on earth had that madwoman said? Had I really heard it? I picked idly at the blades of yellow grass as if trying to solve a puzzle. I assembled the pieces I had intentionally canceled from the last summer I had spent at Roccalba, my grandmother's tears, and even my Uncle Bruno's jokes: "Here we are, dying of heat, and he's enjoying himself in the cooler." The scene of Giorgio Bellusci's arrest floated before my eyes, sharp and cruel, but still tolerable. I kept going, I couldn't stop now. And there it was, the final result of the equation: it was so shocking I couldn't accept it. I jumbled up the answer by tearing up the blades of grass with my teeth and spitting them far away from me.

At home I didn't say anything to anyone, I asked for no explanations. My father was coming to get me in a few days. I was in no hurry. I would wait until I was back in Hamburg, and there I would settle accounts with my mother. She was the one who had betrayed me.

And at first my mother denied everything angrily, "No, no, I tell you no, that's just malicious slander, it's completely ridiculous." She wanted to know the name of the woman who had talked; she called her a witch and a whore, and insisted that Giorgio Bellusci was working in a factory in northern Italy, a shoe factory, in Varese, to be specific. "If you want," she said, "you can go visit him."

I said nothing in reply, but I glared at her with a look of utter disgust. I was furious, and she had told me nothing but lies. My mother hesitated in bewilderment. She stared at me as if I were a stranger. Then she dropped her eyes, unable to meet mine.

Just as she was about to break down, I couldn't take the cloudburst I could see thickening in her eyes, I couldn't take the hand she laid lightly on my shoulder to steady her courage and mine, I couldn't stand to see her heart-shaped lips, trembling and defeated. "You're right," I said to her. "That lady was a bigger turd than her son."

Now I know: I had behaved like someone seriously ill who refuses to hear the truth. Or perhaps my mother's version of things was the truth: in any case, she no longer showed any signs of being in distress, her eyes were clear, her lips were firm, at least for a few seconds, enough time for a hidden, close-mouthed sigh of relief. Then her lips parted, and they spoke to me of how violent the world could be, how evil people could be, how complicated life could become. And if I didn't understand? "One day you will, one day in the not too distant future, and then I'll explain it all to you, in detail. I'll tell you about my father, too, and . . . "

At last Marco joined the conversation; until now he had been playing alone in his room. "*Io will spielen con voi, spielen all'ammuccia*," Marco said in his hybrid language, half-Italian, half-German, a hybrid language I understood perfectly since I had spoken it myself when I was little. He wanted to play with us; he wanted to play hide-and-seek. My mother took him in her arms. "Oh, my, how heavy you are," she said. She ran her hand through his blond curls and, giving him a quick kiss, she spun around like a spinning top.

And then one evening, without warning, my mother began talking to me about Giorgio Bellusci. So the day had come—the day in the not too distant future—when I would have to understand. I listened to her with my eyes closed, because she was talking in a musical cadence that I often liked even more than the stories she told.

Since his boyhood, Giorgio Bellusci has borne the nickname Focubellu because of his restless nature, restless like the dancing flames of a fire. At the age of fifteen, he has a plentiful blanket of downy fuzz under his potato-shaped nose and on his dimpled chin. A grown-up look in his eyes: the two deep wrinkles on his forehead seem to have been carved in with a knife. He picks up the book with its dark brown leather cover and leafs through it with the veneration of an intelligent illiterate. He admires the orderly handwriting with its flourishes, the four roughly sketched maps of southern Italy, dotted with little circles, and embellished with minuscule houses, bell towers, mountains, and rivers. Of course, he can't understand that the little circles mark the legs of Dumas's journey: Messina, Villa San Giovanni, Scilla, Pizzo, Fondaco del Fico; nor can he grasp that he is holding in his hands one of the travel journals written by the hand of Alexandre Dumas, an album, as the writer referred to it. He does, however, sense its importance, and asks his father for permission to catch up with the travelers and return the handwritten book to its rightful owner. It takes an hour to persuade him otherwise: "He'll give me a big tip." "He'll give you a boot in the ass." One more hardheaded than the other.

And it took a few minutes before it dawned on me that my mother really was beginning from the beginning: this Giorgio Bellusci she was talking about was the boy in the sketch done in the Fondaco del Fico by Jadin; his father, behind the counter pouring out the wine, and later arguing with his son, was Gioacchino Bellusci. And by now, the three travelers and Milord have a three-hour head start.

And so Giorgio Bellusci sets off, heading for Maida, where the three men will almost certainly have looked for a place to spend the night. But darkness falls when he is still an hour from the village, and he is barely in time to spot a haystack in the open countryside and take shelter there, until dawn.

That same night, Dumas sleeps in an inn that was described to him as heavenly. Instead, it is a single huge room, filthy, with a loft covered with straw and hay, a breeding ground for rats and mice; even worse, one corner of the room is home to a sow suckling a dozen new-born piglets and grunting menacingly. Nauseated at the filth of the place, Dumas skips dinner and tries to get some sleep, wrapped in his woolen overcoat, perched on two chairs. Jadin lies down, fully dressed, on the innkeeper's tattered cot and, to protect himself against any attackers, holds Milord in his arms. Snoring away on the floor by the fireplace are a prostitute, who had come unasked to brighten the guests' evening, the woman innkeeper, and her brother, a poor "idiot"—as Dumas called him—who sautéed the gizzards of a chicken during the dinner and ate them heartily, turning the stomachs of the two Frenchmen. That was what many inns were like, back then.

My mother grinned ironically at that point in the narrative, and the grin turned a little nasty at the end. It seemed as if she were pleased at Dumas's discomfort. If he had only stayed at the Fondaco del Fico, he would have gotten some sleep that night!

Giorgio Bellusci wakes up hungry. He stretches lazily in the rising sun that rises out the mountains like a bright red mushroom. He blows the dust off Dumas's album and, instead of returning home the way any other Christian would, he continues his journey, looking for a cluster of grapes or an October fig, and especially for the three travelers and their dog Milord.

On the road to Maida he meets the mule driver from Pizzo with just one mount. Giorgio Bellusci courteously asks him where the Frenchmen might be, and the man angrily tells him to go to France, that is to say, to hell, and to take those French oafs with him, because they fired him in the middle of the journey, and now they're heading for Vena with that snarling bastard of a dog, every bit as nasty as the two of them.

That day, in fact, the two Frenchmen reach Vena and Milord mangles an Albanian cat. Yes, because Vena is an Albanian town, like many others in Calabria. The two Frenchmen can tell by the language the people speak and by the women's dress. They are obliged to fork over four carlins for that cat of Albanian origins. There is a silver lining to the story: they persuade the owner of the cat to pose for Jadin in her best clothing. And half an hour later, they stand open-mouthed when she appears in her wedding dress. That insignificant woman who sniffled like a little snot-nosed girl as she hugged her dead cat to her breast now looks like a queen garbed in precious fabrics, covered with gold embroideries.

Later they continue their journey northward into the mountains.

When Giorgio Bellusci arrives in Vena the two Frenchmen are dining on roasted chestnuts again, high above him, an hour's walk away. But his time in Vena isn't spent in vain; Giorgio Bellusci obtains information about the two Frenchmen and their cat-killing mongrel from a group of old women dressed in strange costumes and, in their midst, like a flower in the dry grass, a young girl with light-colored eyes, who lowers her gaze to the spinning wheel she's working on as soon as Giorgio Bellusci smiles at her. The young girl's name is Lisabetta and, a few years later, he will make her his wife.

And so the two-part journey continues: the two wayfarers with the dog Milord climb upward along winding trails threading through an endless forest of chestnut trees; and behind them, Giorgio Bellusci. When they arrive at a high promontory—at different times—they look down upon a view that amply repays them the trouble of getting there: the glittering blue of two different seas, the Ionian and the Tyrrhenian, one to their left, the other to their right. The Gulf of Sant'Eufemia and the Gulf of Squillace seem to have been sketched by Jadin's steady hand, so lovely are they. In that land, the narrowest in all the Italian boot, in the middle of a small plain across which run two riverbeds, they glimpse the Fondaco del Fico and bid it farewell it from afar. The two Frenchmen, forever. If they had a spyglass with them, they could see their innkeeper proudly admiring himself in Jadin's sketch, hanging on the wall, or cursing his son—that blight on his existence!—who hasn't returned home yet.

The boy is exhausted; night is falling; time enough to gobble down a few raw chestnuts and climb a giant oak tree, and then he is already snoring, perched on a huge branch like a wingless bird.

Whereas the two Frenchmen are sleeping in a comfortable bed, lucky souls, at an inn of Tiriolo. Here Dumas, the following day, will learn that the great Vincenzo Bellini has died. Despairing, he reflects on the vanity of life, as he rereads the letter of introduction written for him by his friend Bellini. The letter is still here, in his hands, but Bellini is gone forever.

While Giorgio Bellusci is walking toward the Sila, he feels the earth shift beneath his feet, and he sees people fleeing a nearby village. He asks what had happened; he also asks if anyone has seen two Frenchmen with a dog. The people answer, in consternation: "The village was shaken from top to bottom, son, like a treeful of ripe olives, four tremors, one after the other; all you can see is rubble, stones, and dust." The great earthquake of 1835. But Giorgio Bellusci doesn't turn back. One of the evacuees says that he met those two friendly Frenchmen, and learned that they were heading for Cosenza. "We're going to Cosenza, too," says the man. "At least there they have huts to sleep in."

"All right, the hog is ours now," whispers Giorgio Bellusci, repeating the words his father always said when things were moving in the right direction.

And so, with his new traveling companions, he crosses the Sila without stopping. Finally, in the middle of that day, he arrives at a field full of straw-roofed shacks, surrounded by heaps of rubble, collapsed houses, and damaged buildings: he has reached the ruins of Cosenza. He searches for the two Frenchmen for hours and hours; he walks into open huts, and finds the poor and the wealthy lumped together, barefoot children and ladies wearing expensive hats, dainty veils covering their features. The earthquake forced the entire city to sleep in that field near the Crati River. Everyone there, including Milord—Giorgio Bellusci sees the dog wandering among the huts, in search of aristocratic, well-fed cats to kill. But he can't find the two Frenchmen, Dumas and Jadin. In order finally to enjoy the luxury of a bath, a night in a bed without bedbugs or other repugnant creatures, they have taken rooms at the city's finest luxury hotel, Al Riposo di Alarico. The hotel is cracked, teetering, and certainly dangerous. They are the only two guests, the only reckless foreigners in the entire ghost city of Cosenza.

In vain Giorgio Bellusci continues to search for the Frenchmen. That evening, he eats hot soup with the victims of the earthquake and sleeps in a hut with orphaned children. The next morning, he sets out for home: traveling as fast as he can toward the Fondaco del Fico, without a backward glance. He has done his best to catch up with the travelers, but when travelers are determined, no one can catch them. Indeed, travelers are generally traveling to escape their fellow man. Giorgio Bellusci passes through Vena again; once again, he sees Lisabetta, sitting on the low wall as he had hoped, and with his fiery eyes he promises her that he will soon be back to see her again.

Later, he arrives at the Fondaco del Fico with Dumas's album under his arm, like a tardy student. His father doesn't shout at him, he doesn't even welcome him home or ask him where he's been. Instead, he tells him to come quickly and help him move a dusty beam lying in a corner. The day after he left, two infernal temblors knocked down the roof of the Fondaco del Fico and destroyed the stables. The Bellusci family survived, by a miracle, as had the sketch by Jadin. The roof was rebuilt a few days after Giorgio Bellusci's return; the stables, the following spring.

Now, at last, I thought to myself, she'll tell me about our Giorgio Bellusci, her father the butcher, obsessed with the Fondaco del Fico and cold watermelons. Finally, she'll tell me what he's done. My mother thought she could read my mind. "I know, you must be wondering: how did my mother learn all these stories?" It was simple: she had read Alexandre Dumas's *Le Capitaine Aréna*, and in this book of travel narratives she had learned that, in the fall of 1835, Dumas, his friend Jadin, and the dog Milord had been forced to travel overland across Calabria because a terrible storm had prevented their ship, the *Speronare,* to continue northward. During their travels to Cosenza, they stopped at the Fondaco del Fico. Dumas only mentioned stopping there briefly, but it is certain that they did. He made no mention of the lost album or the portrait of the innkeeper and his family. Nor did he mention Giorgio Bellusci,

also known as Focubellu, the story of whose journey was handed down in the family from generation to generation, all the
way down to her, Rosanna Bellusci, my mother, who was doing
everything she could think of to steer the conversation safely
away from the topic of Giorgio Bellusci, her father.

When I saw Hans Heumann again, I had the unpleasant feeling that I was in the presence of the most arrogant person on earth. It wasn't so much the things he said, the cutting or sarcastic opinions about those attending the opening, including my father, whom he dismissed as "a good little banker with a nice family, who has everything he needs, including a station wagon"; it wasn't even the stream of self-adulation that he spewed like a giddy drunk—for that matter, he had been drinking spumante nonstop since the beginning of the opening of his retrospective show at the Kunsthalle. I understood that the judgments and the self-praise were a provocation, and not even a particularly serious one, given his carefree tone of voice. The arrogance that he was emanating was concentrated in his eyes. His eyes had an irritating color, a brushstroke of light grey and bright sky-blue, seemingly identical to my father's eyes, but if you looked carefully, much more powerful: Hans would turn those eyes on people with the effrontery of someone who knows that no one would ever have the courage to spit in his eye. That man was my grandfather! My same blood ran through those arrogant eyes and that forked tongue! Oh, *Scheiße*! I didn't want to believe it. A sudden thought snapped my eyelids open, as if someone had sneakily jammed a pin in to hold them that way: I was the ultimate point of arrival for that old gentleman, bald and tall and skinny and arrogant as he was, dressed in denim trousers and a denim shirt to make himself look younger; for him, and for another old man, whose appearance I could just barely remember but who must have been another son of a bitch in his own right, now certainly rotting away in some Italian prison, even if my mother would never have admitted it. What a rich mess my chromosomes turned out to be, what a heady mix of toxic blood was running through my veins! My parents saw only the surface of things, and they liked to boast that they had two very special sons precisely because they had been born to a mixed couple. Marco was overjoyed at his magnificent light-blue eyes. He was already just as pleased with himself as his German grandfather, but Marco could claim the extenuating factor of being just three and a half years old. In that brief instant of clarity, I was intensely envious of my closest friends because of their more normal births, so to speak. They were the children of German parents, period. If I tried to pin down my own origins, I would lose my way like the water of a rivulet in the middle of a desert. And, to make things worse, mine was dirty water.

My gaze must still have been locked in place by the pin of that thought, too big for me to handle, because Hans Heumann noticed my discomfort, and asked me: "Is it my pictures that are terrorizing you?" He had an agreeable voice. I reddened in embarrassment, coughed, and answered like an automaton: "No . . . sure . . . the pictures are very nice . . . congratulations . . . sir."

Hans Heumann laughed in genuine amusement. "Sir, my grandson calls me sir, that's a rich one." He looked at me affectionately, his gaze washed clean by a rain of tenderness. Now I could see that he had my father's eyes and I smiled up at him without fear. "Tomorrow, I'll come to your house for lunch, and we'll have a chance to talk without hurry, we'll take all the time we need," he said, stroking my face with the back of his left hand. Then his young wife swept by like a gust of cool breeze and dragged him off to greet more-illustrious guests.

For a while I watched Klaus as he peeked at the photographs with one eye, wandering back and forth in the large hall. With his other eye he was spying on his father, and I was sure that he would have given anything to see him acting a little less distant than usual, even on this special occasion. After that, I was impressed as I watched my mother: unhurriedly she was keeping after Marco as he flashed around the room, moving rapidly from one place to the next. She strode with the posture of a fashion model, her prominent lovely bosom, her long dark legs made even slimmer by her very high heels, her smile of satisfaction at the many eyes admiring her, dressed in a brand-new white outfit, as if admiring an exotic landscape. It wasn't hard to see: my mother stood out among all the women in that huge hall—even the women who looked out at you, coyly, sadly, or alluringly, many of them nude, from Hans Heumann's photographs—because she glowed with a warm light.

In the car I demanded that she sit in the back, between me and Marco, while my father drove, smoking and talking uninterruptedly about the evening, as excited as a little boy who had just been to the circus. When his father said good night to him, he had hugged him the way a father does a son. It must have been ten o'clock by then. Marco had fallen fast asleep, and I pretended I was nodding off, too. I laid my head on my mother's knees and let her stroke my hair until we pulled into our garage.

The next day was a Sunday. Marco and I ate breakfast in front of the television; we could hear our parents' voices from the kitchen as they continued to talk about the inauguration while they prepared a Sunday dinner in honor of Hans Heumann: a Calabrian antipasto with prosciutto, *nduja* (a creamy, spicy sausage), pickled peppers and vegetables, baked lasagna, stuffed eggplant, and a fruit tart.

At exactly noon, Hans Heumann rang our doorbell. My mother smoothed her skirt. Klaus straightened his tie and ran his outspread fingers through our hair as a final brushing.

Hans Heumann swept into the house like a tornado. He was alone.

Hélène was waiting for him at the hotel; she was packing their bags. In less than an hour they had to catch a flight to Paris. He apologized for this hasty farewell. He never even took off his overcoat. He drank an aperitif without sitting down. And he talked, without pause, for ten minutes. We stood, too, in silence. He skipped from one subject to another, like a sprinter running an obstacle race. He had an appointment he had forgotten in Paris, it couldn't be put off, a television interview; the show had been a disaster, mounted without taste or feeling; it seems as if incompetents are always in charge of things in this world; next time we'll have more time to talk, I promise you, Florian; for now he had brought me a catalogue of the show and an envelope full of money—buy whatever you like, I didn't have time to shop for a present for you, and I didn't know what to get, unfortunately we don't really know each other that well; another envelope full of money for Marco, his little Marco; you really look awful, Klaus, why don't you take a holiday with your boys; you look wonderful as always, Rosanna, my compliments; the light is what I care about, not the subject; give my regards to your father, if you go to see him or you write to him, don't forget; the way light is born and moves and dies is what I care about; Hélène says I have two wonderful grandsons; incredible: they should have built a monument to your father, and instead they keep him in prison; the next show is in Paris; I'm tired but happy; there is no such thing, in this world, as justice.

And, just as quickly as he had come, he was gone.

"All that tension and work, for nothing!" was the first thing my father said. He was bitterly disappointed. I looked at my mother; she was not so much disappointed as angry. "That man," she said, "is an asshole. Now, who's going to eat all this wonderful food I've made?"

"Me, mamma, me!" It was Marco's sly, charming, hungry little voice; he was trying to cheer up my mother, inconsolable for reasons only she and I could understand.

After the plentiful but silent Sunday meal, I withdrew to my bedroom. I lay down on the bed and opened the catalogue. At first I focused on the turgid nipples of the five or six naked women in the photographs, nearly all African women. Then I started to be drawn in by their eyes, by the light that glittered in their eyes, cartwheeling through the landscapes and skies, shaping the clouds and transmogrifying them into mysterious beings. You didn't have to be an expert to understand that Hans Heumann was a great photographer. Those pictures wrapped you in a sweet atmosphere of melancholy, and, sometimes, they filled you with disquiet. If you stared at them for a long time, you could hear in your head a heartbreaking melody in the background, like the music from a romantic movie. When my mother came in, I was admiring the photograph of a young Giorgio Bellusci with the dog Milord at his feet; behind him was the cavity-riddled dinosaur tooth: the Fondaco del Fico.

My mother sat down at the head of the bed and glanced at me, fearfully; I responded—and instantly wished I hadn't—with a sardonic grin.

The day had come when I was to learn the truth, in intricate detail, just as she had promised me. There wasn't even a word of preamble. She spoke in her usual melodious tone, but it seemed out of place given the context. And as my mother sang her story, I felt as if I were being enveloped again in the soggy heat of that damned summer; the burnt butcher-shop door flashed into my mind; I saw the sheep and the herd dogs, throats slashed, hanging from the fence; I savored the taste of the rooster's crest of that huge ice-cold watermelon; I remembered how it had made me get up repeatedly to pee in the night.

The next day, in that late Sunday morning in July, the powerful car parked right in front of the new butcher-shop door. It was a nice white Mercedes; just like the ones so many emigrants to Germany drive. This time, the driver got out. He was a stocky, bald man, and he looked about forty. He was alone. He pushed his way into the butcher shop forcefully, banging the new aluminum door. He came to a stop in front of Giorgio Bellusci, squaring up in front of him. He came up to Giorgio Bellusci's shoulders, yet he looked him straight in the eyes, his own eyes shot through with furious fine veins.

"So, hard man, you get the moral of the story? Is one lesson going to do you? Hand over the money and you can go back to your shitty little quiet life, with your shitty little family—we won't touch them, we won't lay a pinkie on them. And, be our guest, build all the hotels you want. But pay up, or else we'll be building a nice hotel for you, one for travelers to the great beyond. Got the idea?"

Maybe it was because the man had insulted his family, or because he had mocked his great dream, or a disproportionate reaction, prompted by instinct; or perhaps he had already made his decision the morning he saw his slaughtered animals hanging from the fence. The metal meat hook, sharper than usual, stuck in the flesh between the stranger's throat and chin; the blow was powerful and accurate. A guttural cry of pain filled the air, as if the man were retching, trying to vomit without success. The man's hands flew up to his throat, thick dark blood streamed down his arms. He was about to slump to the floor, either weakened, or else unconscious, or perhaps already dead, but Giorgio Bellusci swiftly caught him under the arms. And again, powerfully and accurately, he lifted him and hung him on the white tile wall, right next to the last unsold sheep.

Giorgio Bellusci was spattered with fresh blood, and stood there shivering with cold, between the two corpses—man and sheep. That was the scene that greeted the elderly woman shopper who entered the butcher shop, running late that Sunday morning: she screamed so loud that dozens of men came running in from the neighborhood bars and cafés, and they all saw the scene; none of them could believe it. No one in Roccalba could believe it, not even the carabinieri, not even Giorgio Bellusci himself.

My mother licked away the last few tears that pearled on her heart-shaped lips like tiny transparent pimples. She looked like a wounded puppy, and she moved her tongue with the caution and deliberation of a wounded puppy. I threw my arms around her, and felt on my neck the last few breaths of that poisonous air that for years had surrounded the shame she felt at her imprisoned father. Her father, the murderer. Finally, she managed to smile and placed two loving kisses: one on my forehead, the kiss of a grateful mother; the other, the kiss of a loyal daughter, on the shining image of a young, smiling Giorgio Bellusci, his long hair tossed by the wind, like a beautiful savage.

SECOND JOURNEY

My mother, too, was beautiful when she left for Hamburg, the first time: her hair was long and wavy, black as night; she was petite but well-built, with a prosperous bosom and slender legs, not to mention her heart-shaped lips, full and reddish-brown even without lipstick, and had I been my father I never would have tired of kissing them.

Throughout the long journey she never stopped thinking about Giorgio Bellusci, her mother, her sister, and the Fondaco del Fico. She had left Roccalba right after Epiphany, her suitcase filled with books, her college diploma in her handbag. She had graduated from Rome University, with a major in languages, with four years of German; her thesis was titled "Friedrich Leopold von Stolberg—Stolberg and the Grand Tour." This Stolberg had traveled in Italy at the end of the eighteenth century, and he had published his account of the journey in epistolary form, before his close friend Goethe had published his. Of course, she could have done her thesis on Goethe, as her professor had recommended, instead of on this count, illustrious man of letters, great scholar, diplomat, and friend of Klopstock, Claudius, Herder, and Voss, but of whom no one had ever heard. She had picked Stolberg for a personal reason. Stolberg left Hamburg on 2 July 1791 and stopped at the Fondaco del Fico on 22 May 1792, at midday, just like Dumas. Goethe could not make that claim, and there-fore, to her, Goethe did not have stature of "her" great Stolberg.

Back home, her father was sketching out plans on the grey butcher paper he used to wrap the meat he served his customers. He had lots of ideas, he told her, but he couldn't risk it yet, his younger daughter still needed his help, his money in the post-office savings account was barely enough to build the reinforced concrete skeleton of the new Fondaco del Fico, and he refused to go into debt, even to achieve his greatest dream. But he hadn't given up; on the contrary, he was more determined than ever: inside of him the Fondaco del Fico existed already, and it was growing like a wild plant, one of those that manage to grow in the crannies of stone walls, with no more than an occasional drop of water and a couple of crumbs of soil, but which becomes the most beautiful plant of all. All that really mattered, her father used to say, was not to uproot plants like that; everything else comes with time, the plants will grow, they'll outlast life's earthquakes, as long as the roots are healthy and full-blooded, like those of the madder plant.

She had been lighthearted when she left. At last, she could earn her own living; and, with some sacrifices, she could send her savings to her father. But then, when Praia a Mare and the island of Dino went by outside the train window, she felt a lump in her throat, a lacerating pain in her chest. One day in August, she had gone on an excursion to that stretch of coastline, together with her friends from Roccalba. They had sailed a boat around the tiny island of Dino, venturing into the Grotta Azzurra and the Grotta del Leone, where they had screeched out their names like lunatics. Then they had sailed through the Arco Magno and they were in paradise. It was a solitary little beach, with incredibly fine black sand and turquoise water. Above the rock arch, you could still see the cobblestone road built by the Romans and high above, in the dome of the sky, a boundless sun gleamed down. Together, soaking in the cold water that paid them back for every minute of the hot sweaty journey, they swore a romantic oath, vowing, in their naïveté, "We must never leave this land; it is the most beautiful place on earth."

But one after another, her friends from that outing had left, along with everyone else her age; some went to northern Italy, others went to Germany. For work. Now it was her turn. One month and twenty-five days as a substitute Italian teacher in Hamburg, the city from which both Stolberg and Hans Heumann had made their departures: her first job, that's how you get started.

At the Stazione Termini in Rome, while waiting for the connecting train, she made a round of phone calls to the many friends she had met during her four years at university. "I'm going to drown myself in the Elbe," she joked. "but I'll resurface, you'll see, I'll be back." Inside her, the lump in her throat was growing, kilometer after kilometer.

For that whole night she lay there in her berth, her eyes staring at the train window. Dark, light, light, dark, the train ran into and out of nameless stations, implacably lapped up the miles. Every so often, on the screen of the train window, she would glimpse a memory in black and white, a smiling face. The day of Pasquetta, Easter Monday, when she and her sister were little girls. A swing that touched the sky. Chasing each other around the Fondaco del Fico. Her parents, kissing with their lips puckered up, like little children in love. Her father's smiling face. He was telling her the story of Focubellu and Dumas, no question about it; but his voice was drowned out by the train whistles and screeching brakes, she couldn't understand a word, only those prolonged intolerable wails.

The next day, exhausted from her long sleepless night, she stepped down onto the platform in the Hamburg station, and was hit by a snowball. The snowball had been thrown by a blond idiot named Monika.

When my mother told me about her arrival in Hamburg, she often accompanied the story with photographs from the time. They were not as artistic as Hans Heumann's photographs, but I liked them all the same. The eye of the photographer was the loving eye of my father. The subject was Rosanna, young and beautiful, even when a bad-tempered wrinkle sullied her brow, arched her dark eyebrows, and slightly wrinkled her luminous eyes. The young Rosanna lived with Monika, the German friend she had met in Rome. Shortly after her arrival, Rosanna made a comment that would long be remembered: "I couldn't live in this city even for a month." She had never seen so much snow in her life, half a meter deep, maybe more, whiteness as far as the eye could see, a blinding, surreal whiteness. The following morning, out in the street, she felt herself suffocating under the weight of all that snow, and the white sky, and she reiterated her judgment: "I wouldn't be caught dead living here."

One year later, she was living in Hamburg, married and pregnant. She had been chained hand and foot to German soil because of me, she used to joke; actually, she had few regrets, she would have made that journey again, she would have fallen in love again, she said seriously, even though my father had been a turd from the minute she met him. But, for her, "turd" was a compliment, and was more or less the equivalent of a "lovable rogue." If she wanted to offend someone, she would say "certified turd." In short, she was supposed to stay in

Hamburg less than two months, no longer, but in that time something she could never have imagined happened instead.

A few days after she arrived in Hamburg, she went, accompanied by Monika, to pay a call on Hans Heumann, her father's photographer friend. That man, really, that name, had captured her imagination ever since she was little, and perhaps it was on account of him that when she went to the university in Rome, she majored in languages, studied German, and tried to make friends with all the Germans she met, including Monika, who had brought her all the way to Hamburg. His address was written on a piece of yellowed paper: *Hans Heumann—Regentenweg, 24—Hamburg-Dammtor (vileta blanca a 100 metri da Konsulato italiano)*. Her father had taken it out of his wallet and handed it to his daughter with a nostalgic look: "If he's still alive, give him my best wishes and tell him that in Roccalba we'd welcome him with open arms!"

It wasn't hard to find Heumann's *vileta blanca*, or to make it through the front gate. With her melodious voice, Rosanna said that she was an Italian girl who was desperately seeking (that's exactly what she said, "*verzweifelt*") Herr Heumann. The lock buzzed and the gate swung open. At the end of a tree-lined walkway, the girls saw a tall thin man waiting for them at the door of his home. "Herr Heumann?" asked Monika. "*Höchst persönlich*," the man replied, and asked the girls to come in and sit in his parlor. He sat down as well, and courteously asked the reason for their visit. He waited for the answer with an extended, impatient smile. He was bald, just as Rosanna expected, but his face was unlined and his light-blue eyes were youthful; for Signor Heumann, she thought to herself, enchanted, time had stopped after that journey her father had told her about so many times. He looked like a man of forty, not a day older. Young Rosanna was very excited, and barely managed to introduce herself: "My name is Rosanna Bellusci and I am the daughter of Giorgio, Giorgio Bellusci, the man you traveled with in Calabria twenty-five years ago. You remember, don't you?"

Heumann burst into ear-splitting laughter. He laughed for a few minutes like a true lout; this was no German gentleman! "Forgive me, forgive me," he finally said, hands on both cheeks to stop laughing, "you've mistaken me for my father. You're looking for Hans Heumann, aren't you? I am his son, Klaus Heumann. I am sorry to disappoint you, but my father is fifty years old, and I am just twenty-four." He turned serious. "My father no longer lives in this house," he said, "and he hasn't for many years."

Rosanna wanted to drop through the floor. She was embarrassed, red-faced, and she felt like an idiot. She wished she could just disappear. She knew that Monika would make fun of her for the rest of her time in Hamburg and would tell the story to all her friends. They would laugh at her, just like that cretin Klaus had laughed. She didn't like him, either; he was an almost completely bald twenty-four-year-old who looked like he was forty, think of that! An oafish German who laughed as uncontrollably as a drunk on the streets of Roccalba. Rosanna stood up brusquely: "Pardon the intrusion, Herr Heumann," she said, staring straight at him with her dark-brown eyes, squinting slightly in a show of ferocity. "Good day!" She headed for the door, walking with brisk, quick little steps, while Monika continued to laugh, sprawled out on an easy chair. Klaus ran after her and laid his hand on one of her arms. "Wait, please, wait a moment," he said, and touched her for the first time. "Forgive me for laughing just then." He felt an electric shock and pulled back his hand, in consternation.

More than two months went by. They hadn't seen each other again. Suddenly, after Rosanna had returned to Roccalba, Klaus Heumann showed up at the Bellusci home and began courting her. Two weeks later, he brazenly asked her to marry him, and that same night, and every night for the rest of his stay in Roccalba, he slipped secretly into her bedroom— my mother told me this detail, too—and stayed until dawn, never getting out of bed, even to go get a drink of water. They drank each other's saliva. Kisses, kisses, and more kisses—my mother even told me these details because, she said, I was a friend to her, not just a son, the only real friend she had in all Germany.

When they got married, in Roccalba, as Rosanna had demanded, Hans Heumann didn't attend. He sent a telegram from Madrid with his congratulations and best wishes. Klaus wept during the religious ceremony and afterwards, too, at the wedding banquet in a restaurant overlooking the sea. Everyone thought it was because the moment had deeply moved him. Instead, he was crying with the sorrow of finding himself alone in the world during an important occasion of his life: without his mother, who had died when he was a boy; without his father, who was traveling around the world; without a relative; without a friend.

To a certain degree, I envied my father, because he had suc-ceeded in conquering my mother; and yet, at the same time, I pitied him when I thought of him being married without par-ents and without friends. I would have gladly talked with him about all this. I would have liked to hear his version of how things went. But he was always shut up in his "domain," as my mother called his study, piled high with papers and books; I only saw him at dinner, and I was glad to leave him to Marco, who told him about his day at school. In the evening, before going to sleep, I knocked at the door of his study, two hesitant raps. I would immediately repent and, without opening the door, to avoid disturbing him, I'd say: "*Gute Nacht, Papi.*" And he would reply, without interrupting his typing: "*Gute Nacht, Schatz.*"

"Then, one evening in June, I decided to go find her." That is what my father said one evening during a New Year's Eve party at our house. He was drunk and he had an audience of cheerful friends around him. And in a corner, I sat listening, secretly taking in his version of the facts.

That evening in June my father was watching "The Godfather" in a movie house downtown, with a blond college student named Betty. More or less halfway through the movie, Al Pacino escapes to Sicily and, intent as he is on his duty to pursue a vendetta, perhaps he doesn't even notice the huge sky hanging over the sparkling sea and the prickly pears lining the dusty roads, or the despairing song of the crickets hidden in the leaves of the olive trees. But young Klaus, at the sight of that luminous landscape, felt suddenly drunk, even more than now, when he was telling the story, as drunk as if he had downed a bottle of whisky. It was the same dazzling light he had seen in his father's photographs. Later in the movie, when Al Pacino meets the dark girl and not only notices her beauty but falls in love with her and is married to her within the space of just a few scenes, my father was seized with a yearning to set off. And when the dark girl finally undressed to background music that gave him goosebumps, and the cunning eyes of Al Pacino feasted on the firm, virgin breasts, yearning to be kissed by his lips, young Klaus got an enormous erection. He laid Betty's hand on his lap and as she pulled her hand away, after whispering in his ear, "Klaus, you are a pig," and then nestled against him as he wrapped his arms around her, he was admiring the warm eyes of the dark girl and perspiring: *Oh Gott*, how she could smile with those eyes, how well she succeeded in being at once timid and sensuous. And it was then that he was surprised to find himself thinking of Rosanna, as heartbroken as if he were helplessly in love, as if he had never had anything else in mind than her dark image, identical to Al Pacino's Sicilian bride. Strange? It was crazy! How had that girl appeared in his life, a girl that he had seen only once, for a few minutes, two months before?

At the point in the movie when Al Pacino returns alone to America, Klaus left the movie theater on the pretext of a splitting headache, indifferent to how *The Godfather* would end, and equally indifferent to how his relationship with Betty would end. The only regret he felt concerned Rosanna, whom he had allowed to slip through his fingers as if he were an idiot.

The city felt as if it had been plunged into a giant pot of soggy broth. As he walked, he had trouble breathing. What a disgusting city, he said to himself, what you need is pure air, a sea breeze, leaves rustling in the wind. Leave, Klaus, leave. Otherwise your heart will melt in this stinking oven.

A few passersby turned to stare at him. He was talking to himself and gesticulating like Al Pacino.

And so he set out for a village about which he knew nothing more than the name, Roccalba, and some basic directions to reach it: it was south of Rome, in the narrowest part of the Italian boot, on a hill between two seas. He crossed all of Europe north to south, at a hundred and fifty kilometers an hour, thinking of the expression on Rosanna's face when she saw him again.

And finally he came to that blinding light, he stood beneath that vast sky, he saw the sea glittering to his left and the prickly pears lining the dusty roads, he heard the despairing song of the crickets hidden in the leaves of the olive trees, and he recognized his father's footsteps, which—without meaning to—he was now following. His eyes captured the sights, like a series of photographs, and once he was in the countryside around Roccalba, he did not fail to note the partly scorched wall of the Fondaco del Fico rising out of the briars.

Giorgio Bellusci was happy to make the acquaintance of Hans Heumann's son; he resembled his father to a striking degree. Rosanna, on the other hand, leveled her dark-brown eyes straight into his face, squinting slightly, with great ferocity, just as she had in Hamburg before fleeing. Then she spoke to him in German, a phrase that at first extinguished all the joy that had lit up his face: "I'm pleased to see you, you turd." And she kissed him on both cheeks, brushing her lips lightly against his.

"Sorrows, like dirty laundry, should be washed in the family." And my mother, after teaching me this adage through her actions, for many years carefully avoided talking to me about her sorrows, the dirty laundry of Giorgio Bellusci, and even of the Fondaco del Fico and Roccalba.

Then one evening, she came into my bedroom. She looked straight into my face with her eyes like those of a Mediterranean bird of prey, and, with a carefully rehearsed voice that issued from her heart-shaped lips and slalomed around a series of sobs on the verge of breaking free, she said to me in German: "*Florian, mein Schatz, sag' bitte nicht nein!*"

She paused. My mother was begging me not to say no! I was baffled. I sat there, helping Marco to assemble my old toy train, and almost without realizing what I was doing I had begun to play with him, making "toot-toot" train whistles and announcing trains as they pulled into and left the station. I couldn't understand. I waited for her to continue, and in the meantime I worked the toy track switches. My mother spoke to me in German when she was trying to catch me in one of her devious traps. Otherwise, she always spoke to me in Italian, a language that I had learned to speak with her Calabrian accent and cadence, along with her colorful and juicy manners of speech. She went on: "I need you to come with me to Roccalba for Christmas. I need you, I need your support, don't make me go alone."

I could feel the power of her eyes focusing on my lips as if she wanted to pry them open, and the feeblest answer that I could come up with slipped out in Italian: "Me? For Christmas in Roccalba? Why don't you go with Klaus? He's your husband."

It took only a second for my mother to shatter my idea to pieces: "Your father? He's nothing but a stack of paper, with a square computer monitor for a head and a pair of deranged little eyes that still don't know the Berlin Wall came down a long time ago. Don't make me laugh! I said I want support, I want help . . . do I have to get a guitar and serenade you? I don't want someone with their head lost in clouds of files!"

I couldn't argue with that! Klaus was increasingly involved with his work at the bank. When he came home at night, he greeted us fondly but couldn't wait to shut himself in his domain, to write reports, pamphlets, and articles on the best way to build a house with bank mortgages, or how to obtain bank financing for a socially beneficial undertaking. Only rarely, on weekends, would he go to the movies or eat a pizza or take a stroll with us. He had a great passion for his work, and passions, of course, can make you forget about the outside world. But I didn't condemn him the way my mother did. With me he wasn't so much absent as discreet. Whenever I needed him, he would emerge from the half-light of his domain and lend me a hand. My mother didn't even really understand the concept of discretion! She was so indiscreet that she once asked me if I made love with Hannelore, the girl I was dating during this period. She asked me with sincere nonchalance. And with the same nonchalance that day she summed up: "Forget about your father, he's not made for the active life. You, me, and Marco will be leaving in exactly one week. I already have the plane tickets."

It was more than I could take. She had already decided everything. Marco was dancing with joy, but I was smoldering with rage, on the verge of exploding, while she acted like nothing was wrong, smiling while every now and then she let her eyes glint shamelessly, as if everything were settled now. I couldn't understand why we had to go right then, and she didn't try to explain it to me. We hadn't gone to Roccalba together for the holidays in eight years and, now that I thought about it, she had been the one to put an end to that chapter, after her father's arrest, perhaps because she was ashamed. Every so often, her yearning for home would hit her in the pit of the stomach. She was good at recovering, however, and every summer she made sure we took our holidays in places reminiscent of Roccalba: little Spanish or Greek or Turkish villages, with narrow lanes winding up through the white houses, under an incessant mantle of muggy heat, with the scents of basil, garlic, and red peppers wafting out of the open windows.

Now, after years of a tacit truce, here she was breaking my balls—me, of all people, who had been happiest of all about the change in destination, after all those summers spent panting in the murderous damp heat of Roccalba.

Klaus came out of his study at just the right moment, that is, just when I was about to hurl myself at her and wrap both hands around that velvety smooth throat of a forty-year-old woman in excellent shape; he spoke to my mother with his usual calm, and then he turned to me and said, with a broad smile: "This is just wonderful! You'll have a vacation in a different season. Think how beautiful Calabria must be this time of year! If I could only afford to take a vacation, I'd go in your place."

So there was no way out. My only choice now was to throttle them both. Or the coward's way out: go to Roccalba with my mother. Or, in impotent fury, storm out of the house, slamming the door behind me.

My anger lasted only until a gust of cold wind hit my face like an open-handed slap: I regained my senses, I felt alive and happy. I decided not to think about my mother's idea anymore, to keep from ruining my evening: a birthday party, at the house of a schoolmate of mine. I'd see my friends, I'd savor my world as I kissed Hannelore. The other world, my mother's world, made me break out in a cold sweat every time I remembered its existence, or whenever I looked at the letters that Martina kept writing me, even though I never wrote back. Dear Florian, I really miss you. Dear Florian, I love you so. My beloved, why don't you ever write me? Dear Florian, the years pass, but my love for you only grows. My love, when will I see you in Roccalba again? That girl was as stubborn and pushy as my mother. Sentimental, too, just like her.

And, in fact, when I got home that night, I found my mother in front of the television set. She was watching a romantic movie by herself. She was moody and apathetic, as if she were suffering just as much as the actress sobbing on the screen, as she watched her husband and his lover leave the house, slamming the front door behind them. My father was working in his study; Marco had been asleep for awhile. That atmosphere of desolation left me depressed. Or maybe it just struck me as desolate, because I was coming home from such a lively and noisy setting.

I felt a lurching thump deep inside, like when you drop too fast from the twentieth floor in an elevator. My filial love revived; I offered to make her a cup of chamomile tea, but she had already made one. And, with her hands wrapped around the steaming mug as if she were holding onto a warm buttress, she subtly shifted the subject to Christmas in Roccalba, the huge bonfire they build in front of the church, a sight I should absolutely not miss. And since I was listening attentively, she continued to talk about herself, about when she came back from Hamburg, the first time. She was relaxed, and enjoyed telling the story. But just when she got to the most interesting part, she changed her tone of voice and the subject. As if, from her deathbed, she were announcing her last wish, she whispered: "Well, Florian, have you made up your mind? You can't tell me no. I want you to come with me."

I couldn't withstand her clear-eyed suppliant gaze: I dropped my head and, at the same time, nodded yes.

The whole way down in the airplane, I played cards with Marco; I almost always let him win, because whenever he lost, he thought up excuses, and even claimed I had cheated; he was likely to burst into tears if I contradicted him. My mother was reading an Italian magazine with a look of ecstasy. It might as well have been a prayer book. Though perhaps she wasn't even reading it, maybe she was just warming her heart in anticipation, considering that her return home would be no simple matter.

Just before we landed at Fiumicino airport in Rome, she pulled herself away from her magazine and looked around in annoyance. She said nothing during the flight to Lamezia, as if the trip had dried up her tongue.

We got to the airport of Lamezia at five in the afternoon; my aunt and uncle and Teresa were waiting for us with an umbrella. It was pouring rain. My mother and Aunt Elsa cried up a storm, and it seemed like they would never stop hugging. I had never seen it rain in Calabria, and it stunned me, as if I had made an important discovery. All the while, Marco held tight to my overcoat, a little cowed by his mother's and aunt's hysterical sobbing and by his cousin Teresa's kissing and hugging. This was the first time she had ever seen him. I could scarcely recognize her myself; she had become a flourishing young woman, not unlike her mother when she was a girl. Aunt Elsa seemed to have put on weight, or at least that's how it struck me as she stood next to my mother, who still had an excellent figure. "Drenched sisters are lucky sisters," said

Uncle Bruno, "but enough is enough; you'll catch your deaths." And he pushed them both into the car.

Aside from the incongruous rain, as soon as Uncle Bruno's Fiat Tempra pulled into Roccalba, I felt as if I were returning after a year's absence, that is, after the same lapse of time that passed between my childhood visits. The village had spruced itself up, the houses were in better repair, the streets and the piazza were paved with little cubes of porphyry, but everything looked familiar, the sensations I experienced were the same as ever—a slight sense of numb bewilderment, caused this time not by muggy heat but instead by the driving rain.

I embraced my grandmother in the kitchen and once again felt the softness of her lovely humps, which had become if anything rounder and larger with the years. She was enveloped in a little cloud of basil, oregano, and rosemary scents, and when she lifted the lids of her pots and pans, the aroma of her cooking burst forth like a steam geyser from a volcano. Now my bewilderment was truly pleasurable, and it took me back in time. Inevitably, I thought of Giorgio Bellusci. I saw him walk into the kitchen's white light, one long-ago summer, with a huge watermelon on his shoulder and a ghostly smile. We all moved toward him in greeting. Now, in contrast, no one had even pronounced his name. Not even my mother. At dinner, however, as she sat facing her father's empty chair, her eyes began to film over, while her heart-shaped lips twisted in spasms of uneasiness. For a moment her eyes filled with tears, but perhaps it was just because of the spicy *diavolicchi* that she was eating.

The next day a tepid, almost springlike sun peeked out. Everyone who came to see us began the conversation by saying, "Welcome back, you've brought nice weather with you." Then they continued with rhetorical questions: "And who is this handsome young man? Who is this pretty little boy? And this lovely lady who never looks a day older?" My mother would answer for Marco and me; she had become talkative again, and, as the hours passed, the volume of her voice crept upward to match the loud, loud voices of her fellow villagers. Her hand gestures and facial expressions changed, too, in an aggressive mimicry, so that at first Marco watched her in fear. He couldn't understand the Roccalba dialect and was afraid that she was arguing.

I reassured him, and he quickly over came his shyness and mistrust. Then, as time passed, he started to realize he had arrived in a little earthly paradise, where all the adults were saints; they brought him toys or coins; and the local children competed to win his affection and play with him.

At two o'clock, Teresa came home from school. She leaned over and spoke into my ear: "Look, she's waiting for you outside."

I understood and hurried outside. Martina was waiting for me, leaning against the veranda railing. When she saw me, she came toward me and extended her hand. The handshake you give an acquaintance, of course. What was I expecting, for her to jump all over me? She was wearing a short skirt and a mustard-yellow leather jacket, beneath which throbbed her pert, small breasts. She was fine-boned and petite, prettier than I remembered. But I was disappointed at the wintry pallor of her face, though it was enlivened by her large, intense green eyes and a cascade of glossy black curls.

We walked together along the Corso Roma. Every so often, some stranger would greet me, introducing themselves as a relative of my mother, or a childhood friend. Martina was astonished that I didn't remember anyone. "That's not true," I said, to flatter her. "I remember everything about you." She gave me a stern look; maybe she didn't believe me. So I changed the subject and I began pelting her with heartfelt questions. I learned that she was in her junior year of high school; her father had suffered an injury on the job, and now he had a limp and a pension; her sister was married and worked in Switzerland with her husband; she, Martina, had no boyfriend, had never had one, admirers, sure, lots of offers, but a real boyfriend, a potential fiancé, never, and I—she told me—should understand why. To my relief, she made no mention of her letters, because she wasn't trying to make me uneasy.

We walked past the last house in Roccalba, and for a while we strolled along in silence. We went past the sports fields and turned onto a dirt road that ran through a grove of Holm oaks and on to a small public park, recently built. I was happy to see these new things and, as we talked, I could feel the fresh air of the woods filling my lungs. We came to a clearing that had a picnic area, with benches and slides for children to play on. In the middle of the clearing was a little lake, shaped like an hourglass, with water the color of clay. Dotting the surface of the water were dead leaves and bark from the rough wooden fence poles that surrounded the park. You could make out sad little goldfish moving through the water sluggishly, despairingly, as if they were expecting the end of the world to arrive at any moment. I felt that they had been condemned to a cruel fate, sentenced to a loneliness without possibility of escape; instinctively I wrapped Martina's warm hand in mine, like a frightened child. Martina interpreted my gesture the way she chose, and said: "I've missed you too, so much."

Now I felt as if I were watching the whole scene from a comfortable seat in a movie theater, rather than experiencing it myself. The woods opened out slowly before us as we walked; a robin sang somewhere as if spring had arrived, the stream ran peacefully along in the ravine below us, and Martina's eyes were the same rich green as the Holm oaks. I could sense the warmth of her lips even before I touched them with my own.

On Christmas Eve, I went back with Martina to the little lake in the woods. It was a place we both liked: silent and deserted, an ideal spot to talk and kiss. We brought bits of bread to feed the goldfish, live worms that Martina stole from her father, an amateur fisherman, and, for their dessert, a slice of *panettone*: they seemed to enjoy it. They seemed more active, wriggling and darting, more alive, perhaps even happier. "Like me," I said to Martina, and I admitted to her that I was happy during that holiday in Roccalba, because of her.

At home, there was a buzzing and a hubbub, a busy festive air that I had never seen before. The women were caught up in preparations for the traditional thirteen-course Christmas dinner, and Marco was telling everyone who would listen that he was going outside with his friends to gather bits of scrap wood that all the families would throw on the big Christmas Eve bonfire. The boys had been at it for more than a month, he said, gathering wood, sometimes with wheelbarrows, and in the last few days the grownups had started to lend a hand, bringing Holm oak trunks or the roots of olive trees and oaks into town from the countryside by truck or tractor. All of this had captured Marco's imagination; he would gladly have spent the rest of his life in Roccalba, gathering firewood.

After the Christmas Eve feast, our bellies swollen as if we were pregnant women, we walked over to the square in front of the village church to watch them light the bonfire. The wood was piled high, and Uncle Bruno told me that it would burn all night, well into the next day. In that still night, the fire was burning slowly, spreading and burrowing, like an enormous red-hot drill, into the mountain of dry firewood.

Martina showed up with a gang of kids just before the pealing bells announced that Mass was beginning. My family entered the church and I devoted myself completely to Martina. I talked to her about the Christmas Eve bonfire: this was the first time I had ever seen it, but my mother had told me about it all my life, so often that it seemed familiar. I talked about her: we had spent the whole afternoon together, watching our goldfish in our figure-eight lake, but by nightfall I already missed her terribly. I held her hand and looked into the bonfire with a tenderness that seemed completely unlike me. Then I glanced over and noticed a cab that had just stopped on the other side of the flames. A single passenger got out, with a heavy military rucksack slung over his shoulder; the weight made him stumble; he nearly fell. The crowd clustering around the bonfire watched him curiously. The stranger was tall, slightly hunched over; his face was hidden by a broad-brimmed summer hat and a long, full, grey beard that spread upwards to cover his cheekbones. He wore a dark, lightweight suit that was much too big for him and a white shirt with a rumpled collar. At first I didn't recognize him at all. He looked like an elderly tourist who had just arrived from somewhere in the southern hemisphere, unaware of the fact that in Italy the twenty-fourth of December is wintertime. He walked over to the fire, lowered the rucksack to the pavement and, ignoring the buzz of voices, young and old wondering who he might be, stood staring into the flames with an ecstatic expression.

It was a majestic bonfire. When the cab pulled up, half of Roccalba had been standing there looking up at the roaring flames that leapt as high as the bell tower, and the sparks that crackled and flashed in all directions, only to be devoured by the insatiable darkness. Now the old man had captured the attention of the crowd, and he had in turn taken the fire for himself as if it were his lover: he reached out to caress it with his hands, and then rubbed them together vigorously, he let the fire warm his face and his whole body, he stretched out his arms to the flames, and even let it warm his curved back, turning slowly around as if he were performing an old-fashioned dance. The night was cold and dank, so no one thought that he was crazy, not even the children and young people who watched him in amusement, not even the old people, people his own age, renowned for their hasty judgments and their meaness. Instead, everyone watched him and wondered who he could be, asking one another who that man who had pulled up in a taxi might be; his face looked familiar, we must have met him sometime, somewhere, who could say, but one thing was certain, the old people agreed, he wasn't an emigrant coming home from Bonsaire—the local pronunciation of Buenos Aires. When they came back from there, they traveled with steamer trunks, not little rucksacks like that one: it held almost nothing. They were such gossips, so nosy! I couldn't stand them. Taken alone, maybe they were all right, men with old-fashioned ideas, but straightforward enough; but get them in a crowd and they were as noisy as cicadas, more tiresome, intrusive, an invasive crowd of chatterboxes. Still, I was curious myself about that old man—curious and uneasy. I stopped gazing lovingly at Martina, stopped rubbing her warm breasts with my elbow, and now I stared through the fire at the stranger dancing slowly with its flames.

Martina told me that I seemed to have fallen into a trance; now that I had stopped moving, she began rubbing her breasts against my warm elbow.

Suddenly I felt myself shiver, even though the combined heat of the bonfire and Martina could easily have melted a rock. I knew who that man was, and a rolling thunderclap in the distance tore through my heart. There he stood, the reason my mother had insisted on taking this trip, no matter the cost. I hadn't known that Giorgio Bellusci had served his sentence; I had assumed he had been given life without parole.

No, no, they must have given him life without parole, of course they had, so that man dancing with the fire wasn't him, I thought hopefully, pushing the thunderclap of revelation out of my mind: it's just some old lunatic who thinks that winter is summer, that Roccalba is Rio de Janeiro, that the Christmas Eve bonfire is Carnevale; and I'm as crazy as he is for listening to thunderclaps inside of me, instead of focusing on the lightning bolts darting out of Martina's eyes, this girl who is burning to kiss me, her nipples straight and hard, about to explode, and if I don't take her tonight to the house that her emigrant sister has left empty, she'll give me a kick in the ass and I'll never see her again.

It was just a few minutes before midnight, and I whispered in her ear my plans for the Blessed Night of Christmas: "Let's get out of here, when the bells start ringing—nobody'll notice a thing, they'll be too busy wishing each other Merry Christmas. What do you say?" And just as she began nodding her head, my eager confederate, her curls bouncing, the old man stopped dancing. He threw his arms into the air in a dramatic gesture, and shouted happily: "Don't you know who I am? It's me, Giorgio Bellusci. Giorgio Bellusci! Don't you know my voice? Sure you do! It's me, it's me. Giorgio Bellusci, in the flesh. I'm back among my people; back to see our Christmas Eve bonfire. I've come back to you!"

And when the bells began pealing to announce to Roccalba that the Christ Child was born, Giorgio Bellusci continued to talk, even more emphatically, becoming ridiculous and generous: "I am reborn, today I am reborn, here among you, in my own Bethlehem. Drinks for everyone, on me! Young people, go to the bar and bring cases of beer, orangeade, and Coca-

Cola, bottles of cognac, it's all my treat. On me. Giorgio Bellusci!" And the bells were pealing, the crowd was clapping, applauding the birth of the Christ Child and the rebirth of Giorgio Bellusci, the festive crackling of the bonfire, we were all laughing and wishing one another Merry Christmas, shaking hands and kissing cheeks, as the first cases of beer and the first bottles of brandy were opened and handed around; everyone Giorgio Bellusci's age was clustering around him, hugging him in surprise and curiosity, thumping him on his stooped back to see if it was really him, really there in flesh and blood.

"Your grandfather's returned, Florian! Aren't you going to welcome him back?" Martina asked me. I didn't answer her. I pretended I hadn't heard her, hadn't understood, nothing had happened; you have a perfect alibi, I said to myself, uncertainly, hold out, be strong, don't go hug that man even though you ought to, don't ruin your Christmas Night.

"Florian, what's the matter with you? That's your grandfather. He's come back." Martina kept asking me if I was going to go over to him. I wished her Merry Christmas and finally I embraced her, holding her as tight as I could.

"I'll say hello to him later. Later," I whispered in her ear. I wanted to run away, with her or by myself, to the ends of the earth, far from Roccalba and especially from Giorgio Bellusci. I saw my mother burst out of the church, pursued by my grandmother, Aunt Elsa and Teresa, all running in single file toward the bonfire, elbowing their way through the crowd and flinging their arms around Giorgio Bellusci's neck. I took Martina by the hand, and we snuck away into a dark alley, slipping our hands under each other's clothing and our tongues into each other's ears, moving toward Martina's sister's house, uninhabited and therefore chilly. We would be able to heat that house with our own little fires, eighteen-year-olds that we were. That man whom I couldn't call Grandpa, even in my mind—I'd say hello to him at home tomorrow morning. Unwillingly.

*

I kissed Martina for the last time at four in the morning, after walking her back to her house, in front of the big main door. That endless night of fire and surprises had worn me out.

I walked stumbling, my feet were soft as ricotta, my head was buzzing. In the distance I saw the smoldering remains of the Christmas Eve bonfire, burnt down from a magnificent mountain of flame to a hillock of hot embers. Sitting on the church steps were grouplets of young people, talking, drinking, smoking, and warming themselves by the hot coals. I decided to avoid them; I was afraid somebody would say something embarrassing about Giorgio Bellusci; I took the long way around, walking down narrow lanes reeking of dog piss. I pissed on the wall of a garage myself, a long, loud piss. A few minutes later, I went inside.

I didn't even turn on the light; I didn't want to wake my family. I moved as cautious as a bat, soundless, almost breathless. Everyone was sleeping, or at least that's what I thought at first. Then, from upstairs, where my grandmother slept, I heard a smothered moan, like a dog in pain. It was hard to resist the temptation to eavesdrop; I slipped off my shoes and crept up the cold marble steps. A line of light shone through the partly open doorway; I could take a look, as well as listening. I swear, that wasn't my style, but that moan really was unusual, and most of all I was curious to see old man Bellusci sleeping with my grandmother after seven-and-a-half years.

I thought they would be snuggling in their sleep, maybe weeping in emotion! Not exactly! The two of them were making love, big time! Giorgio Bellusci—stooped, pale as could be and even skinnier than with his clothes on—was digging his fingers into my grandmother's chubby body, and he was screwing her like a pro, licking her big, still-springy tits, tits that heaved as she panted just like Martina's. Well, I'll admit it, I never would have guessed that a pair of old people could make love with that sort of passionate vigor; it captured my imagination. Deep down I did my best to feel resentment, jealousy (for my grandmother), and disgust, but it was a Catherine wheel of fakery that withered in the face of that seething passion in the dim light. When my grandmother turned around, her ass in the air, and Giorgio Bellusci began to mount her like a frenzied colt, I realized I had gone well beyond the bounds of common decency, and I withdrew to my bedroom.

As I lay in bed, I heard them groaning for at least another hour. Then, finally, sleep washed over them, sweeping me along with them into slumber.

My mother dragged me out of bed at ten that morning. "Your grandfather's back, you can't sleep like this, wake up, Grandpa's here," she kept yelling. And she pushed me, still in my pajamas, into the living room, where the whole blessed family, on the blessed morning of Christmas Day, was cooing over Giorgio Bellusci as if he were a swaddling baby. Expressions of fondness, kisses on his forehead and his pink lips, hugs, loving and joyful whispers came pouring down on the leather easy chair, the one that had been covered for years with a linen sheet, the little throne where no one had even been allowed to sit before this day. Giorgio Bellusci, who was a prolific dreamer, may have dreamed of this outpouring of welcome many times while he was in prison, but he seemed surprised by it; the smile in his heart lit up his freshly shaven, rejuvenated face. *"Buongiorno,"* I said as I came to a halt in front of the leather throne, and, in embarrassment, I yawned.

Giorgio Bellusci was wearing a pair of black corduroy trousers and a red turtleneck sweater of mine. The youthful clothing, the clean-shaven face, the glittering eyes of a man who has just spent the night making love made him look like the son of the man dancing before the Christmas Eve bonfire. Even his back was straight now.

"Nice manners!" my mother scolded me. "Go welcome your grandfather properly." And since I continued to stand there, awkwardly, she shoved me into his arms.

"Florian, oh, Florian," Giorgio Bellusci sighed, deeply

moved, and then he hugged me and pecked kisses at me for a couple of minutes. "*Carissimo* Florian, what a handsome young man you've become! Let's see how tall you are! You're taller than me! Luckily, you didn't take after your mother in height; she's a midget. But you're as good-looking as she is in every other way. No question about it: your mother made a pair of masterpieces, little Marcuccio and Florian, the two handsomest grandchildren in all of Roccalba—in the whole world! Come here, Marcuccio, come give me a hug, and you, too, Teresa, what a pretty *signorina* you've grown into, lovely as a movie star, like your mother when she was a girl. You don't even look like your father's daughter. And my daughters, come to me, girls; I'm so proud of you both."

Uncle Bruno did his best to smile at his father-in-law, but he would have throttled him if he could; my grandmother, on the other hand, was glowing with joy: her husband was home, her family was together, that night together . . . She clearly could hardly believe her loving eyes.

I broke free of the clustering crowd and sipped at my cup of coffee. Giorgio Bellusci wouldn't let me be: "Florian, oh, Florian, what a strong, smart, clever young man. They tell me you're in high school, that you're a good student, always bringing home good grades. School is a great thing, you know. Where I've been, till now, I got my junior-high-school certificate, and I read more books than your high-school graduate of an uncle here ever dreamed of. Tell me, tell me, boy, do you have a girlfriend? With that Zorro mustache of yours I'll bet you do." Finally, with a wink, he whispered in my ear: "Get as much pussy as you can, Florian, as much as you can, later you'll regret every chance you let slip, don't let any of them get away." Everyone could hear him, even the women, and Marco was the only one, just seven years old, to burst out with a dirty laugh.

I offered nothing but smiles in return, after the *buongiorno*

I said yes a couple of times, ahem once or twice, and once a *grazie, grazie mille*. I heard Marco saying the word *nonno*—grandfather—over and over, as if he had said it all his life; he talked to Nonno Giorgio, telling him about the Christmas Eve bonfire, about flying in an airplane, about how he could always beat me at cards. Luckily Giorgio Bellusci listened to him, clearly grateful to Marco, he coddled him and praised him, even. He never noticed my silence. Later—during and after the meal—he never even noticed I was there, because the house filled up until it was as packed as a bar, crowded with men and women, mostly the same age as my grandparents, but younger relations, too, even young men and women, and children, drinking shots of amaro, whisky, brandy, drinking beer and orangeade and soda pop and fruit juice; drinking and hugging and kissing and whispering to him, the same words and best wishes, over and over again till you were ready to vomit: how are you? fine and you? me too, you haven't aged a day, no neither have you, just a few white hairs you didn't use to have, just a few teeth missing, but we've missed you, and I missed you all, you're looking spry as a young man, so do you, thanks, certainly, and you? how about you? me too. They would laugh, forced laughter, and sometimes they would clearly be moved, chancing on the name of someone who, Lord bless us and keep us, had passed on, to a better place, a better life. No one mentioned the years in prison, no one referred to the brutal murder that Giorgio Bellusci had committed. Of course, they were being tactful, discreet, letting the past lie; or perhaps it was cowardice, fear of upsetting, even for a moment, the "courageous murderer," as the newspapers had described him at the time. It almost seemed as if they were greeting an old emigrant who had come back from America after twenty years away. But Giorgio Bellusci was nothing like the old *mericani*, there were none of the old nostalgic plunges into the village of his birth, into the spicy flavors to be savored for the last time, the graves in the little graveyard in which to rest in peace for all time. Giorgio Bellusci had come back—and I would soon understand this fully—had come home to resume his life at the same bloody point where he had been forced to break it off. Or, at least, to try. He was weirdly serene for a man who had just spent many long years in prison. At least, in appearance. No one else could know what was in his mind but he. He would plunge his hand into his rucksack and, with a broad smile, distribute to his guests packets of cigarettes, nylon stockings, chocolate bars, packs of chewing gum, tiny bottles of liquor, *panettones* the size of a fist, nougats and candies, miniature red Ferraris, the very latest model. And so the tide of people slowly ebbed, flowing out of the living room or the kitchen, clutching what Giorgio Bellusci called *"un pensierino"*—a little gift, a small keepsake—and out into the street, to the village square, to the bars, to the homes of their relatives, to call on others and say Merry Christmas; and as they did, some of them, far away from Giorgio Bellusci and his intimidating gaze, would tell the younger people or outsiders just what Giorgio Bellusci had done to deserve all that time in prison.

When I finally decided to leave the house, I found Martina and her friends in the main square, talking about Giorgio Bellusci. They referred to him respectfully as *zu* Giorgio, uncle Giorgio. They seemed to know almost everything about him, and some of them, including Martina, spoke of him as a courageous man, "a man with balls." In fact, said one law student with a great show of expertise—a young man that the others already called Avvocato Arcuri—Giorgio Bellusci had been sentenced to eight years in prison despite the fact that he had perfectly legitimate mitigating circumstances: he had been the victim of threats and violent attacks. But the court had chosen to focus only on the aggravating circumstances, the fact that he had killed the man with such cruelty and had then inflicted further insult on the corpse, hanging it on that hook on the butcher-shop wall, as if the man were a sheep newly slaughtered. There was another consideration, added Avvocato Arcuri: they couldn't just release him; it would have amounted to an admission that people had to take justice into their own hands. And the Italian state didn't want to give that impression.

I was baffled; what should I say? That I wished one of them had Giorgio Bellusci for a grandfather, instead of me? They could keep their hero. In just ten days, I would be far away from him and from Roccalba. And, unfortunately, from Martina, too. That last thought depressed me, and Martina could see from my expression that I wanted to be alone with her. She made an excuse to get away from her friends and together we went to see our goldfish, and kissed until nightfall.

At dinner, Giorgio Bellusci did everything he could to make himself likable and appear happy to be home at last. And yet I sensed a note of menace that I couldn't understand. I studied him carefully: his teeth had yellowed, his complexion was a sallow olive hue, and when he rubbed his closed eyes with his fingertips he struck me as a very sick, tired man. As soon as he opened his eyes, though, they glittered continuously and savagely, like the eyes of a horse about to break into a frantic gallop.

He didn't even wait for the holiday season to end. He went out and started working in the fields on Saint Stephen's Day, the twenty-sixth of December. That evening, he came home in a hot fury at Uncle Bruno, swearing that his son-in-law had reduced his garden of Eden into a hellish bramble of thorn bushes, underbrush, and weeds. It had grown up around the Fondaco del Fico, swallowing it up and suffocating it. The olive trees had shaggy foliage, like a bunch of unkempt longhairs, and their branches were even starting to become tangled with the branches of the fig trees, the San Giovanni pear trees, and the Japanese medlar trees. It was a glaring jungle, it seemed out of place, impossible to believe. And the prickly pears! Prickly pears were growing everywhere, huge, dense, arrogant masters of what had once been an enviable piece of farmland; it was now nothing more than a prickly-pear farm. "If you take a look you'll find are prickly-pear bushes growing out of your asshole," he shouted at Uncle Bruno. "Are you blind, didn't you see what was happening? Didn't it break your heart to let good farmland go to waste like that? If you didn't want to trouble that big fat belly you've been cultivating, you could at least have hired a day laborer; you would have made money in the bargain; that's great land and everyone envies us for it."

Uncle Bruno defended himself with the same words he had yelled a few days before at my grandmother, when she begged him to do something about the land, which was collapsing in ruin: "I do all I can. I'm not a farmer, you know. I'm an office manager; I do the job the way I'm supposed to."

"A dickhead is what you are," replied Giorgio Bellusci, who had never been able to stomach this son-in-law of his. "When I die, that land will belong to you. It's your duty to keep it clean, orderly, the way you'd take care of a child."

I felt bad for my uncle. It had been a rude, uncouth attack, but, after all, Giorgio Bellusci had a point. Uncle Bruno was lazy. He would venture out into the countryside a couple of afternoons every month, on the way home from the insurance office where he worked. But the next day, and the day after that, he would take a nap in the afternoon, and then he would go to the bar to play cards with his fellow office workers. What was worse, he was a proud and mistrustful man: he wouldn't even rent the land out to a farmer, because he was afraid he would be taken advantage of.

Giorgio Bellusci swallowed a mouthful of wine and remembered the state of the grapevines. "Not to mention the grapevines," he finally said. "The vines have been left untended, like twisted sheep turds, shat out all over the place. I would have broken down and wept when I saw them, but it goes against my principles. In any case, from tomorrow on, and for the rest of the holiday, you're coming with me to work out there. I'll show you how to eat bread."

Uncle Bruno turned pale in anger. He said: "If you think you've come back to rule the roost, you're sadly mistaken." He stood up from his meal and left the house, slamming the door behind him.

The next morning though, he was the first one up. And he tried to wake me up too, at six in the morning. "Come along and give us a hand; it'll be fun," he said. I could hardly keep my eyes open. I had spent the night with Martina, at her emigrant sister's house, and I had only been in bed for a couple of hours. But I didn't want to refuse; it seemed rude. It was just that my body refused to obey even my best intentions, the blankets were heavy as lead, my legs and arms were like rocks, I couldn't move. And Uncle Bruno was shaking me roughly to try to get me out of bed. "C'mon, get up, come with us." He was begging for my help, he wasn't really ordering me to get up. My uncle just didn't want to spend a whole day alone with his father-in-law. And it wasn't hard to understand. Luckily, just as my limbs were beginning to obey, I heard the voice of Giorgio Bellusci saying to his son-in-law: "Let the boy sleep. I heard him come in at four in the morning. He'll help us some other time."

But in the days that followed I came home in the wee hours and Giorgio Bellusci could never bring himself to wake me up. I was grateful. I was worn out. I would spend the afternoons with Martina, strolling along the Corso or at our park; in the evenings we'd go with our group of friends to eat a pizza or go to the movies, in town. Then I would take her home and wait, hidden in a dark lane, until her parents had gone to sleep and she could leave the house, the keys to her sister's house in hand. And as I waited, and the minutes dragged on into hours, I would begin to boil. When we were finally in bed, and I could explore the length and breadth of her body with my lips, like an inexperienced traveler who had fallen under a spell, I realized that Martina was much prettier than Hannelore; warmer, too, and in love.

One afternoon, though, Giorgio Bellusci herded me into the front passenger seat of his old, iron-grey Simca automobile. "Let's go out to the Fondaco del Fico," he said. Sitting in back were my mother and Marco.

"I want to show off the first phases of the renovation, before you leave," he added, and without thinking, I asked, "What renovation?" Giorgio Bellusci looked daggers at me. Behind me, I heard my mother and Marco whispering and laughing.

"What renovation?" Giorgio Bellusci parroted me, incredulous. "Everyone in Roccalba has been talking about it; they're talking about it in other towns around here; even Marco knows about it, and he asks me: What renovation? Are you really a donkey or are you just imitating one?" He parked next to a bulldozer. "He's a donkey, he's a big donkey, grandpa," Marco answered for me, dancing around our grandfather. Giorgio Bellusci hushed him, and pointed with his index finger across the blacktop road, toward the open clearing of clayey soil carved out of the dense overgrowth of olive, fig, and pear trees, like the protruding tongue of a naughty child. We walked toward it, silently. My mother held her father's hand. She was the most deeply moved of any of us. The ruins of the Fondaco del Fico waited for us in the silent countryside. We could clearly see its unbroken perimeter, consisting of shards and blocks of masonry of varying sizes. Rising above all the shattered masonry was a tall and almost intact façade, the jagged stone wall, bigger than I remembered it, finally freed of the welter of thorns and trees that once suffocated it. In the middle, among the glittering light-blue stones, there was a vivid brushstroke of green: it was a young fig tree growing out of the wall.

The day before we left for Hamburg, Giorgio Bellusci summoned me to his big bedroom. "Sit," he told me, and pointed to the chair next to the night table.

We had just finished eating, and a tissue of sleep was weaving itself around me, no matter how hard I tried to fight it off. I would happily have laid down on the bed and slept until it was time to go see Martina. But Giorgio Bellusci kept fluttering around me, with nervous, jerky motions, like a swallow. He took a key out of the night table, walked to the far side of the room, opened the armoire with the key, slipped a hand under a pile of shirts, and pulled out two keys of different sizes. Then he fluttered over to the foot of the bed and, with the big key, opened one of the nine dresser drawers. Inside that drawer was the inlaid wooden box of his dreams. He lifted it delicately, holding it in both hands, and raised it level with his eyes, in the pure white light pouring through the French doors, proud as a king showing his newborn son to the crowd beneath a window. But I was all the crowd there was, and Giorgio Bellusci walked toward me with his treasure in his hands; he lovingly laid it on my knees, turned the small key in the lock to open it, and said: "There, take it!"

A pungent scent of bergamot wafted out of the open box, or perhaps it was just the drama of the moment that tickled my nostrils. I picked up the album that had belonged to Dumas and noticed, as I ran my fingers over the dark brown leather cover, that they trembled slightly. I leafed through it carefully, afraid I would bend or tear a page. On the frontispiece I read the title, inked in block print: VOYAGE DANS LE MIDI D'ITALIE, ALBUM 2, OCT. 1835, and, under the title, in a signature with flourishes: Alexandre Dumas. It was a manuscript of some forty pages, with four crudely drawn maps of southern Italy, filled with little drawings and circles. The last few pages—no more than ten—were blank.

Then it was time to look at the sketch by Jadin. I took a single glance, and I was inside the Fondaco del Fico in 1835, between Dumas busily writing and Jadin sketching. Across from them, motionless but alive, smiled Gioacchino Bellusci and his wife, Diamanta; the daughter was clinging to her mother's flounce skirt, the son stood next to his father, their gazes lost in the shadows of time. The little girl was named Aurelia, Giorgio Bellusci told me; she was ten in the picture, and at age thirteen she died of malaria. Back then, the whole area was infested with vicious mosquitoes, and malaria killed more people than old age, the brigands, and the Bourbon monarchy put together. The boy was fifteen, and the portrait clearly showed that he was strong, taller than his father. In fact, he survived both malaria and pneumonia. He was the last innkeeper of the Fondaco del Fico, but he took his father's place when he was over thirty and married to an Albanian girl from Vena. In town he was known as *Bellusci il fuoco* ("Bellusci the Fire"), or Focubellu, because he flared up at the slightest sign of stupidity; his nickname became his destiny: he would flip open the blade of his jackknife the way he had seen his father do since he was a child whenever ruffians appeared at the Fondaco del Fico; he would swing threateningly at local tyrants, and they would hold their tongues and slip back to where they came from, tails between their legs.

When he heard that Garibaldi had crossed the Strait of Messina and was marching on Naples, he went to meet him with six strong young men from Roccalba; he joined

Garibaldi's Thousand in the town of Curinga, where General Garibaldi had spent the night as a guest of the Bevilacqua family. It was late August, 1860. At first, it seemed like a festival: wherever they went, Maida, Tiriolo, San Pietro, Soveria, Rogliano, Cosenza, or Castrovillari, people applauded and the women knelt, kissing Garibaldi's hand. Then, around October, the first fighting: blood was being shed, his friends were dying around him, and Focubellu was always in the front lines, with his well-honed bayonet. He came back to Roccalba around Christmas, even more fiery than before, after the Kingdom of the Two Sicilies had been conquered.

Under his management, the Fondaco del Fico prospered. It was always full; locals and outsiders frequented it all year round. Even the local brigands would come by to eat there in groups of ten or more, while a pair of brigands stood guard outside the main door and another kept an eye on the stables. The brigands paid like any other customers, even though they had muskets resting on their knees, and murderous gazes. They respected Focubellu just as he respected them. They weren't friends; you couldn't say that. But he had known many of them all his life: they were young men from the surrounding areas, a few them of them were even from Roccalba, and they had chosen to become brigands rather than being drafted into the army in northern Italy while in the south their families starved to death, rather than handing over years and years of their lives to a king they had never seen, rather than dying for this unknown monarch. We're talking about some of the brigands; others, if a spade is a spade, were criminals, born, bred, and fed, brigands in the worst sense of the word, that is, thieves and killers. And so the king of Italy sent his army down into Calabria to erase the brigands from the face of the earth; the war that followed was brutal, as everyone knows, a war between brothers, bastards on both sides.

One day in July, 1865, a peasant—tempted by the reward

that was offered to anyone who provided information leading to the killing or arrest of a brigand, an enormous sum for the time, 8,500 lire for a brigand chief and 2,000 lire for an ordinary brigand—this treacherous peasant, then, alerted the soldiers of the Italian National Guard that a band of brigands was celebrating, with their chief, at the Fondaco del Fico. They were celebrating an ambush that they had laid for a platoon of the Royal carabinieri in the vicinity of Pizzo. They had killed three carabinieri and they had taken their weapons, ammunition, and horses. They felt safe at the Fondaco del Fico; they were drinking and toasting, and every one of them was drunk, except for the lookouts. When the brigands inside the inn heard a hail of shots and the screams of their fellow brigands on guard, and then the heavy thumps of their bodies falling to the ground, they knew that they were surrounded. Suddenly everyone fell silent—brigands and the national guardsmen; the only sounds that could be heard clearly were the chirping of the crickets and the twittering of the last few swallows; as is well known, in good weather, the swallows swoop and turn in the sky until late at night, catching gnats. Finally, the commander of the national guard spoke up; just a few words, in Italian, but clear enough: "Surrender and come out with your hands up; you'll never get away!"

The brigands knew that they had no chance of escape. After killing those soldiers that morning, if they surrendered they would be executed by firing squad on the spot, and even Jesus Christ Himself couldn't do a thing to prevent it. So they might as well start shooting back, and hope for a miracle, or at least die fighting, having sent a few of these bastard dogs from Piedmont to hell ahead of them. The brigand chief sent out Focubellu, his Albanian wife, and their two young daughters, with their hands up. He also sent out a young brigand from Curinga who was shitting in his pants, trembling and weeping like a child: "I don't want to die," he moaned. "And who wants to die?" shouted the brigand chief, and shoved him out into the open with a kick to the seat of his pants. Then an exchange of gunfire began that reduced the walls of the Fondaco del Fico to a sieve and tattered the bark of the trees all around the inn, killing two soldiers—but not a single brigand was hit. After that, the national guard commander had an evil notion, an idea that made Focubellu's fiery blood run cold in his veins. He ordered his soldiers to take the bundles of dry sticks from the stables and pile them all around the walls of the Fondaco del Fico.

Focubellu shouted into the wind: "Don't do that; stop! It's wrong, sooner or later those brigands will surrender anyway. There's no reason to do this: you're burning my inn, you're destroying my life."

The officer in command responded by gesturing to his men, who immobilized the furious innkeeper, and then set fire to the sticks in a number of different points at the same time. Then he said: "Don't worry; as soon as the brigands see the fire, they'll come running out, and we'll put out the fire."

The first thing to catch fire was the stable, filled with straw; it went up in the blink of an eye, the fire devoured it in a single flaming gulp. The brigands knew they were done for; they began shooting wildly, firing through the flames that had raced around the Fondaco del Fico in an instant, and were now settling down to gnaw contentedly on the venerable portico and the window frames made of seasoned walnut, the trees next to the outer walls, the tall fig tree and the poplar, the mulberry trees and the Japanese medlars—the bastard flames were lapping hungrily with their tongues of fire. Everyone expected the brigands to come running out, hands up, through the gaps in the wall of fire, but instead they continued to fire. Those shots were wasted, they never hit a soul, and the flames danced merrily, unhurt by the bullets that sailed through them.

Suddenly, the shooting ceased and silence fell: what had

happened? What game were the brigands playing now? The only sound was the crackling of the creeping tongues of fire, the deafening roar as the first beams crashed down onto the flimsy wooden tables covered with empty glasses. Then the roof collapsed onto the second story, caving in on the bedrooms, and the middle of the floor gaped open, tumbling downward, and carrying with it furniture and beds, doors and windows, beams and walls. The fire was put out suddenly by the collapsing rubble—the external fire, that is—but beneath the little mountain of smoking stones, in the cellar underneath the Fondaco del Fico, with its barrels of wine, its huge jars of olive oil, and its stacks and stacks of firewood for the winter, the fire continued to burn fiercely, and the brigands all burned alive, screaming like livestock at the slaughterhouse, louder still, and praying for death to come and take them.

If there is such a thing as hell, that's what it must be like.

"There's no need even to bury them," said the commander of the Italian national troops. "They saw to their own burial. You, sir, don't despair. You will be reimbursed down to the very last cent. I give you my word of honor. You will be able to rebuild your inn, better than it was before."

Focubellu managed to break free of the soldiers' grip; in a single feral leap he was at the commander's throat, and he tried to claw out the officer's eyes. He would have done it, too, if four or five soldiers hadn't attacked him. They tied him up and left him for hours and hours; he never exactly calmed down, but he finally fell into exhausted slumber.

The commander kept his word; the money finally arrived, but not until many years later. Focubellu had died the year before, when he fell down the slippery, sleet-covered steps of his house in town. His head split open like a ripe eggplant. He was drunk every night; he was poverty-stricken and insane.

The Albanian widow was named Zonja Lisabetta; she was a shrewd woman. She counted up the money and understood that it wasn't enough to build a single unfinished story of the Fondaco del Fico. Besides, she was afraid of the place by now, with the souls of the brigands screaming underground. So she kept some of the money to feed her family; she gave the rest to her only son, Gioacchino, born when Focubellu was already well along on the road to becoming a drunkard. Let her son buy passage on a ship to *La Merica*, let him go out into the world in search of his fortune, and let him come home safe and sound, with the help of the Madonna del Pollino, to whose sanctuary she made a pilgrimage every year, even after the death of that hotheaded husband of hers, the husband that she alone called by his real name, Giorgio, Giorgio Bellusci, may his soul rest in peace. When he got back, if he wished, Gioacchino could rebuild the Fondaco del Fico: if he wanted, once he was back home, and once she, Zonja Lisabetta, knew he was safe, she would go to join her Giorgio in heaven.

Gioacchino left and lost himself in the distant *Merica Bona*. He never wrote to his mother, and yet he knew how to write; he was lost, perhaps dead. There were, however, people from Roccalba who claimed that they had seen him, on a construction site somewhere in *Broccolino* (Brooklyn), driving a truck, when back in Roccalba there weren't even bicycles, only mules—mules, donkeys, and a cart or two. Then, word spread that he had become a butcher, that he was spending all his money on expensive clothing and corrupt women. He vanished from sight again, and by the time everyone assumed that he had died of syphilis in some hospital, penniless and mad like his father, Gioacchino came back. He had the clothing of a *vero mericano*, there was even a large gold band on his ring finger, and an overcoat with a fur collar for winter. Money, however, not much. Or not enough to rebuild the Fondaco del Fico. And, after all, he didn't seem to be all that interested in that, either. Instead, he opened a butcher shop, purchased a piece of good land down by the river, adjoining the land of the

Fondaco del Fico, and went to find a wife for himself in a distant town, San Giovanni in Fiore, a place that was famous throughout Calabria for its beautiful women. He married a girl named Mariangela, of a poor but honest family, beautiful and sixteen years his junior. In 1927 they had a son, and of course they named him Giorgio. "And that's me," Giorgio Bellusci proudly ended his story.

"And I," he added, after placing his treasures back in the wooden box, shutting the box up in the drawer, and hiding the last key in the bedside table, "I swore, ever since I first learned this story, when I was twelve years old, I swore on the souls of all our dead ancestors, that I would rebuild the Fondaco del Fico. I have never forgotten that oath, even when fate decided to punish me. Now, now that I am finally free, now that I can, no one will be able to stop me."

In the end, he spoke like a deranged fanatic, impetuously, his brow furrowed. Now he stood mute, staring straight into my eyes. What did he want from me?

"Unless someone stops me first . . ." he said.

He fell silent again. But just for a few seconds. And I soon found out why.

"If someone stops me first," he repeated, solemnly, "promise me that you will carry this project of mine to completion."

I was silent. At first I couldn't even breathe. His words had taken me by surprise. What did I care about his dreams?

I tried to avoid the question: "Who would stop you? And why? I'm sure you'll do it on your own."

"Promise me," Giorgio Bellusci shouted, losing his patience. "Promise me, and stop trying to change the subject!"

I'll admit: I was afraid of his eyes, which had suddenly darkened; I was afraid of the words he shouted, which precluded any further hesitation.

"All right. . . if I have to. . . I promise you."

"Okay," said Giorgio Bellusci. "For now, I'll accept this

reluctant promise; I can see you're not convinced. But with time you'll understand, just as I came to understand, that it is a matter of life and death, that you can't say no, that no one can say no."

If I hadn't been able to understand clearly what he wanted from me at first, you can imagine how confused I was by this last enigmatic speech. It would take a psychiatrist to do so, or someone as crazy as him.

At last, he came over to me and tousled my hair with one hand.

"Your hair is turning dark and curly, just like your mother's," he said fondly. "Now go, I can see that you're upset. You have the glazed eyes of a ram. There's some young ewe waiting for you. Get pussy, Florian, get all the pussy you can, otherwise you'll regret it bitterly when you're my age."

I spent the evening with Martina without ever smiling, and she thought that my long face was because I was about to leave. Instead, I kept envisioning Focubellu and the brigands burnt alive in the cellar, I kept thinking about the promise that Giorgio Bellusci had extorted from me. I embraced and kissed Martina with a rage that she mistook for fiery passion; instead it was the fury of the weak, being vented at a safe distance from the claws of the powerful.

I went back to Hamburg like a tourist struggling, even during the trip home, to free himself of his most compromising souvenirs. Of course, I missed Martina a little, but I wasn't suffering. I didn't feel the pains of love, no ineluctable yearning for her, or for Roccalba, or for my grandparents. For that matter, why should I?

Before long, I resumed the life I was leading before Christmas: school, home, discotheque, and even Hannelore, as if the holidays in Roccalba hadn't affected me in the slightest. The detailed and repeated accounts of recent events that my mother and Marco gave my father left me indifferent. And they left him indifferent, too, although he at least pretended to listen—his forehead transformed into a sea of tiny waves dotted with beads of sweat. In reality, he was overwhelmed by an event that he described as "the biggest opportunity of my life." A leading American magazine had commissioned a lengthy article on the new, subsidized mortgages being offered in the principal European countries. He barely noticed that we had come home, and our mother, romantic and in love as she was, took it hard. Worst of all, upon our return the house resembled a pig sty, she said, especially the kitchen: there wasn't a single clean dish, glass, spoon, or even a knife, with which to cut her husband's head off. The only way to get into his study was with a bulldozer—that was his business—but he hadn't aired the master bedroom, not even once; his nose and lungs had become accustomed to that gas chamber; light a match, and the apartment would be blown sky-high, she said. In the face of my mother's vivid imagery, he responded with a tiny smile, like a period: he had no time to waste on that. Full stop.

One evening I took advantage of his profound and enduring distraction to ask him for the car keys. I had had a driver's license for a month now, but he had let me drive the Volvo only once, and in his presence. He tossed the keys to me without even looking away from the dark-blue screen of his computer monitor. I thanked him and went out without saying a word to my mother; she was a worrywart, and she would certainly have stopped me, because it was snowing, it was already late, and at dinner I had drunk two beers.

The long Volvo hugged the snow-covered roads, and often seemed to have its own ideas: sliding and skidding clumsily, startling me. Altona, Reeperbahn, and then the waterfront, the river Elbe, the huge white parks, everywhere there was a blaze of warm lights, translucent snowflakes that, as soon as they appeared with their acrobatic pirouettes, were sucked into the car's bright headlights. Hamburg in the snow was mute and mysterious. I admired its orange lights, and every so often one of them would wink at me, going out or coming on suddenly.

I got as far as Dammtor: on the frozen Alster, dozens of people were ice-skating, despite the still-falling snow and the late hour. I parked; a short while later, I was crossing the river on foot, taking running starts and sliding for a few yards each time. A few days before, I had brought Marco here; in a single afternoon, after plenty of falls and lots of laughter, he had learned to ice-skate halfway decently. My father, who was an excellent ice-skater, had taught me. And so I walked, among the whistling blades and pirouettes of the ice-skaters, who sometimes grazed me with their elbows; I could hear the grating scuffing sound of my footsteps on the snow spread over the ice. It was incredible to think that sleeping beneath my feet were the athletic trout that in the springtime I had seen leaping over the surface of the Alster like tiny dolphins. In the springtime, they were filled with fishy joy, snapping at insects, furiously swinging at the sparkling air with their tough, punch-hardened boxer's snouts. In comparison, the wimpy little goldfish in the park in Roccalba were lightweights, knocked flat by invisible fists in a boxing ring at the far end of nowhere.

I ran from the banks of the Alster River without thinking for a second about what I was doing; I went looking for a phone booth. I had to hear Martina's voice, find out how she was doing, ask if she still loved me, whether she had gone to our park, and what had become of the goldfish.

I furrowed my brow, smiling as I dialed her phone number, and when Martina's sleepy voice asked "Who is it?" I said in a knowing, charming voice: "Surprise! Ciao, Martina. It's me."

She didn't answer. I could only hear her breathing, muffled by distance; it sounded as if she were panting. I went on: "I really missed you today."

She said nothing; instead, I heard her slam the receiver down hard. It came to my ear as the flat report of a slap. I hadn't expected that reaction. I redialed the number. Martina picked up the phone; this time she said, furiously: "You go to hell! I never want to talk to you again. I'm not a whore, to satisfy you whenever you feel like it. You've ignored me for a month and a half. You didn't even call me to wish me happy birthday. You're a bastard, Florian."

Crack: another sharp slap punctuated her angry goodbye.

Well, in a way, she had a point. A very sharp point. I hadn't called her once since I had left, it was true, and I had forgotten her birthday. So what? Who did she think she was, my wife? What did she want from me? She never wanted to see me again? *Bitte.* I found it annoying, but it didn't hurt me, I wasn't suffering. I was proud of myself, proud of my selfishness. I was eighteen years old, with snowflakes on my head. I felt like a wise old man, like Giorgio Bellusci, get pussy, Florian, all the pussy you can, otherwise you'll regret it later. I got back in the car. I made an angry but perfect U-turn. And I drove off fast to Hannelore's house.

Three days later, all that remained from that heavy snowfall was an occasional isolated puddle, by the side of the road. It was the end of February, but a beautiful and unexpected sun shone down as if it were May.

"You Germanians always complain about the weather, but it's nicer here than in Roccalba," said Giorgio Bellusci when he stepped out of the train. The whole family had come to meet him at the Hauptbahnhof; even my father had taken time off from work—he knew that otherwise my mother would hold it against him—a mortal offense—for the rest of her life. Giorgio Bellusci was dressed for a special occasion: beautiful jacket, tie, and a woolen overcoat that he had never worn in Roccalba. He wore a brand new Borsalino hat. He had come to visit because my mother had pestered him relentlessly: three weeks, four at the most, because work on the Fondaco del Fico had already begun, and with him away, who could say what sort of crappy job the builders would do? The time had come, though, to have his missing teeth replaced and see some specialists who knew what they were doing. And his doctors would be part of the Heumanns' family health plan; the costs would be low— my mother sweetened the deal—for medical care that you could only dream about in Calabria.

Giorgio Bellusci put one arm on my shoulder, he took Marco by the hand, and now he was walking boldly toward the train-station parking lot. My father was pushing a luggage cart with all my grandfather's suitcases; my mother was walking ahead, leading the way and talking giddily.

Half an hour later we were home, in the living room, sur-rounded by two suitcases and five packages.

"How did you manage to carry all this stuff?" my mother asked Giorgio Bellusci.

"Me? I didn't carry anything; the train carried it for me," he answered jokingly. Sausages and salami, *nduja*, slices of prosciutto, provolones, cheeses, dried figs, chestnuts, oranges, bottles of sardelles and *giardiniera*, pickled olives, black and white, a jerry can of olive oil and another of wine . . . "How did you manage to carry all this stuff, eh, Grandpa?" Marco asked him too, in admiration.

"Grandpa is strong," Giorgio Bellusci answered him, patting him fondly on the cheek. I looked at him: he looked pale and exhausted. Right then, it looked like only his tongue was strong. And his typical thuggish glare.

We all did our best to help him. My mother took him to the family doctor and the cardiologist, I took him to the dentist, my father took him to the urologist, and Marco took him outside, for walks in the park skirting the banks of the Elbe River.

And so I discovered that Giorgio Bellusci was afraid of doctors. He stared in terror at the needle on the syringe that the dentist was about to use to inject anesthetic in the base of his cavity-ridden tooth; he warded off the dentist's hand in a panic, begging me to tell the dentist not to hurt him. When the time came to make molds of his teeth for his new bridges, his eyes bulged in panic and he started making strange gestures, waving his hands to indicate that he couldn't stand having his mouth clamped shut, that he couldn't breathe: "One more minute and your grandfather would have flown up into heaven," he told me after the dentist removed the mold-plate from his mouth and he could finally breathe deeply again.

Back out on the street, or in the bus or car, he became bold and funny again. It seemed as if he had lived his whole life in Hamburg; he was at his ease, he never had to ask directions, he walked along looking straight ahead. He didn't pay much attention to monuments, churches, avenues, and skyscrapers; instead he stared at women, young or old; it didn't seem to matter, as long as they had "big bazooms."

"Florian, you still haven't told me whether you have a *cervella*."

I pretended not to understand: "What's a *cervella*?"

"A *cervella* is a lady *cervello*, but not *cervello*—the Italian word for brain. It's dialect for she-goat, *capra* in Italian."

"Oh!"

"You brainless twit! You're playing dumb! You're a cabbage head, you are!" And he laughed with his new teeth, finally gleaming white.

At home, before and after dinner, he would play cards with Marco: he had taught Marco all the tricks he knew, both at *briscola*, and in new games, like *tressette*, *scopa*, and French *sette e mezzo*. Whenever the two of them played cards against me and my mother, they were unbeatable, because when luck didn't seem to be on their side, they would cheat like roadhouse gamblers.

"Who do you love better, *Marcuzzo mio*, grandpa Hans Oimànn or your own grandpa, Giorgio Bellusci?" the old cardsharp would ask the child cardsharp.

"What, you have to ask? My handsome grandpa Giorgio Bellusci, of course!" that little brownnoser Marco would answer.

Giorgio Bellusci would laugh contentedly in my father's direction, and my father would smile courteously back at him, even though he hadn't heard a word.

"It's nice here. Or, at least, I like it here just fine. In a way, I hate to go back to Roccalba," Giorgio Bellusci would say, with great sincerity, whenever he turned serious. "But I have to, *ich muss*, as they say in German." And it wasn't because he missed my grandmother, his relations, the village. The real reason was the usual one: "The Fondaco del Fico needs me."

One afternoon in March, Giorgio Bellusci came home twisted with pain. He had just been to the dentist for a check-up; my mother was supporting him by one arm. He was so pale it was frightening. He only had time to put his hat on the little table by the front door and loosen his tie, when my mother screamed in a hysterical voice, "My God, what's wrong with you?" as he slumped to the floor with a dull thud, clutching at his chest with both hands, fingers outspread.

"An ambulance, get an ambulance," my mother cried to me, and then began weeping and moaning, even pulling out clumps of hair, because she understood it was a heart attack and assumed her father was already dead.

As Marco's weeping joined hers, a mournful wailing echoed through the room; our neighbors must have heard it. No one came to ask what was wrong or offer to help. After calling for an ambulance, I tried to stay calm. Was Giorgio Bellusci really dead? Do people really die like that, all of a sudden? Should I try to administer mouth-to-mouth resuscitation; should I try to pick him up, or leave him where he had fallen to keep from doing further, irreparable damage? I began to rage at my father who, at this time of need, was still hard at work, at the bank. I was managing to think, however clumsily, but I couldn't move.

I stood stock-still, I could no longer even hear the sounds of my mother and Marco weeping and crying in despair.

The wailing siren of the ambulance brought me out of it;

the ambulance left, siren still wailing, and taking my mother with it.

I stayed there with my brother and did my best to comfort him, stroking his hair and hugging him close to me. I couldn't actually speak. If I'd opened my mouth, I would have started wailing and moaning, and there's no telling what would have come out next. Soon enough, the pain turned into a sense of helplessness, and the helplessness turned into a massive, inescapable loneliness. No one could help us; we were alone in a city of almost two million people. And, for a while, that thought tormented me more than the fact that Giorgio Bellusci might be dead or at death's door.

At last, after two cruel hours, the phone rang. It was my father; he had rushed to the hospital as soon as my mother called him. He spoke in a frail voice: "Your grandfather is in very serious condition, but, thank God, he survived. It's a miracle. He's alive."

That same evening, phone calls began to pour in from Roccalba: first my grandmother, my aunt and uncle, and Teresa, who had been alerted by my mother, then relations, friends, and even strangers. It was grueling to have to keep telling the same story over and over, especially to my grandmother, who was in despair, as if her husband were already dead. Her bags were packed, she told me, but my mother had forbidden her and my aunt Elsa to come up to Hamburg; they would only create problems instead of helping; Grandpa was being well cared for. In fact, my mother never left him untended; she spent every day at the hospital, and my father joined her when he got off work.

The phone calls kept coming in the days that followed. Everyone wanted to know what had happened, how Giorgio Bellusci was feeling; then they would comfort me, telling me that the worst was over, not to worry, to get something to eat.

One evening Martina called me. She was upset, and maybe

afraid: "Florian? Forgive me if I bother you at a time like this. I wanted to ask how *zu* Giorgio is doing."

"He's better now," I reassured her, "but he is going to have a heart operation; it won't be a simple matter." I was happy to hear her voice, and I didn't hide it. I asked how she was, how school was going, whether she had been to see the goldfish.

Martina thawed as we spoke; she was deeply moved, and she spoke to me in her most loving voice. She hadn't been back to the park since the last time we went together. She couldn't have stood it, she said. She would have cried like a baby. Because, she added shyly, she still loved me.

I felt as if she were half-an-inch from my face, her green eyes brimming over, her breath warm on my ear. All I said was: "Me, too," and I kissed the receiver tenderly, just a few moments before her telephone card ran out.

Three days later, when Marco and I could finally go visit Giorgio Bellusci, accompanied by our mother, we found him imprisoned in a spider's web of tubes, thick and thin, and wires running from his nose or arms or chest, intertwining and tangling in a menacing welter. He smiled faintly and made a feeble stab at winking.

Sitting beside him was Hans Heumann, holding his hand as if he were a child, his head leaning back, in meditation and silence. We stood there in silence for a while, too, touched by the scene. Then we tiptoed out, careful not to disturb them.

When Hans came out of the room, he hugged us each in turn, his eyes glistening and worried. Later, when he learned that we were hungry, he took us to eat at a Chinese restaurant.

I was surprised at how thoughtful and kind he was to us. He insisted that we eat because, he said, we looked unhealthy. Rosanna, especially, was looking tired, he thought. If she didn't start taking care of herself, she'd get sick too, and that was the last thing we needed.

My mother thanked him for the visit, and for a moment it seemed as if Hans were angry: "Are you joking, Rosanna? For an old friend? And I was already in Europe, in Paris, it was no problem. Luckily, Giorgio is no longer in danger. That's what matters."

"Yes, that's true," said my mother, and then she dropped into a resentful silence that I couldn't understand; or maybe her silence wasn't resentful at all, maybe she was just tired and intimidated by Hans.

Marco and I ate ravenously. Hans scooped spoonfuls of spicy sauces on the rice, on the roast duck, and even on his bamboo shoots, in a subconscious contest with my mother to see who could eat spiciest, who could stand the heat.

Predictably, my mother won the hot-and-spicy contest; she could have beaten a fire-breathing dragon. Hans took his revenge with the wine. He drank two bottles of Moselle, justifying his pace—with each glass that he gulped down—by saying that this wasn't a strong wine, "not like the wines you make down in Calabria," he said to my mother. "Three glasses of that stuff will lay you flat on the ground. This is like fruit juice: try some, Marco, a child could drink this." Marco didn't have to be asked twice, and Hans praised him: "Good job, Marco, you're a real man." And now the monologue began. He, Hans, drank, ate, and never got fat, he said; he made love more than a man half his age. He hurried from one place to another, from one continent to another, like a restless swallow, and stress was his daily bread. Everyone expected to see him drop in his tracks from a heart attack, but he kept going; have you ever heard of a swallow having a heart attack? Instead, the heart attack had hit the strongest man in the world. He really had been surprised by the phone call from Klaus; he wished he could have been there that very minute. He had been surprised because, for the first time in his life, he was sorry he hadn't seen him again since that long-ago journey. He'd thought about him, certainly. He owed Giorgio Bellusci a lot. And not just because of that photograph, a picture that had changed his life.

That's when I understood that the wine was starting to affect him. Hans Heumann kept taking about regrets, but his mind wandered in other directions, as if the story he now told had been waiting inside him, and the wine had made it surge to the surface. He had deep regrets about Klaus, too, he said. He'd never given the boy the love he expected. He'd left Klaus alone with Erika, the woman that he, Hans, had loved more than any other. And regret for neglecting Klaus after Erika died in a car crash. Erika was a drinker, a heavy drinker, a profoundly unhappy woman.

He, Hans, hadn't meant to be that way. He just didn't know how to be a father. How could he? He'd never seen how it was done. His own father died when Hans was still in diapers, he couldn't even remember his face. And so his mother, a few years later, when Hans was still a boy, decided to go back to Sweden, to get away from the growing Nazi violence. Hans's mother was from Stockholm, a great woman who had sensed the impending danger long before lots of smarty-pants intellectuals. She had saved her son from bombing, suffering, perhaps death. After the war, she had refused to set foot in Germany again; she said that she never wanted to look a German in the eye again. Her son didn't feel that way. He said that he knew how to tell good Germans from murdering Nazis. And so he returned to Hamburg, in 1947, when he was twenty-two, and found their little "villa" intact amidst the rubble, as if the bombs had avoided it, had known that the owners had nothing to do with that damned war. Why had he gone back? Hans asked himself. That's a good question, he answered himself. Aside from the fact that he was born in Hamburg, maybe he'd gone back to find his dead father. You can run away from the living, but not from the dead. But the problem is: a dead father can't teach you how to be a father. And how could Hans figure it out on his own? Sure, he had tried to get closer to his son, but Klaus had reacted like a little porcupine, a resentful porcupine, filled with hidden rancor, the most poisonous kind. The distance that separated them had only grown over time. "Then you showed up," he told my mother. "You were looking for me and you found him; you were a mother and father to him. Don't say it's not true, it's obvious, even the children can see it. You're a wonderful wife and a wonderful mother, and you're pretty, too: what more could you want? I was happy about his marriage, happy for him, and I'll admit that, from the day he got married, I felt relieved of a burden. I knew he was in good hands. I could suppress my regrets for the rest of my life, I figured. But I was wrong."

Hans was drunk. Good thing the wine wasn't strong, I thought to myself. He managed to walk a straight line and keep from stumbling, though. We accompanied him to the taxi stand, and when he spoke to the taxi driver, telling him to take him to the airport, I saw a glint of arrogance light up his eyes.

We drove home in the Volvo. My mother sat in the back seat, at Marco's insistence; he curled up on her knees and quickly fell asleep.

When we got home, I took Marco in my arms, carried him upstairs, and tucked him in.

My mother was waiting for me in the living room. She was exhausted, *twisted up like a pinch*, as she used to say. I expected her to tell me about Giorgio Bellusci and the heart surgery that the doctors said could not be postponed. Instead, she made herself comfortable, her lovely legs stretched out on the sofa, and pointing her finger like a teacher, said to me: "Don't believe him, don't believe a word of what he said. That Hans is a faker. He has a huge ego, like all artists. He thinks only of himself. What he did, he did because it served his purpose. First he abandoned his wife and son, then he left his son to raise himself, and he enjoyed life as he liked. He has more money than God, and he earns more all the time with a few stupid photographs. Regrets, hah! He was and remains a womanizer. It's his fault that his wife is dead."

The things my mother said struck me as unfair, considering everything that had gone before, and somewhat dishonest. She had written Hans off as an egotistical artist, a money-mad philanderer. But it didn't seem like the time to criticize her; after her outburst, she had slumped back into sleepy fatigue, becoming once again twisted up like a pinch, asleep.

"**M**ilord . . . " That was the first thing that Giorgio Bellusci said when he regained consciousness in the hospital bed, following his heart surgery. He didn't know where he was, he explained later. He was listless and weak as a traveler dying of thirst in the desert of death. Why Milord? Only my mother understood.

Milord had saved his life twice. The first time was during the journey he made as a young man to Bari. The second time, many years later, was one winter evening.

Giorgio Bellusci was returning home, after herding his flock of sheep into the sheepfold. As he walked up a steep piece of rocky road covered with slushy snow, he slipped and fell, like a sledge, all the way down, to the bottom of the ravine. In the middle of the night, when he had not yet returned home, his wife became alarmed, and she reached out to her neighbors. A dozen men set out with flashlights and flaming torches.

By the first light of dawn, they had heard the echo of distant barking: it was coming from the fog-shrouded ravine. The men felt no false hopes: if Giorgio Bellusci hadn't died immediately from the injuries sustained in his fall, he would certainly be dead from exposure after an arctic night like they had just experienced. Two of them ventured cautiously down into the ravine, supporting their weight by grabbing onto tamarisks and broom plants. There was Milord, draped over him like a heavy blanket. The dog had barked and snarled all night to ward off the wolves, it had licked his hands and cheeks, and now it stared feverishly at the two men, it was even snarling at them, a weak, agonized snarl. Giorgio Bellusci had broken one leg and two ribs; he was scratched and bruised all over; but he was alive and warm, as warm as if he had slept in a bed alongside his wife.

"Milord . . . " Giorgio Bellusci said again.

When we came back to visit him that evening, he seemed wide awake and even lighthearted. "It would be horrible to die far from home," he said slowly. "And it's not time for me to die, not yet. I have a thousand things to do, I don't have time to die now." He did his best to grin at me, but he could only muster a grimace of pain.

The next day, I went to pick up my grandmother at the airport; I took her directly to the hospital. "Here he is, safe and sound," my mother said as soon as she saw her. My grandmother delicately embraced her husband. She wiped away two tears that she had been unable to keep in, and looked him over from head to foot: "Lord Jesus, you look bad. How do you feel? Giorgio, tell me the truth."

Giorgio Bellusci answered: "Now that I see you, I'm fine. I feel like I'm thirty again, with the smell of you in my nostrils."

"Klaus never said beautiful things like that to me," my mother commented with a smile. My grandmother blushed like a teenage girl.

When Hans and Hélène came to visit us, Giorgio Bellusci had left for Roccalba a week earlier. He had spent a long time at our house recuperating, coddled affectionately by everyone in the family, and especially by my grandmother. Giorgio Bellusci had undergone a difficult bypass operation; my mother, daughter of a retired butcher that she was, explained the operation as follows: "They cut his sternum open with a saw, and they inserted a vein they took from his leg, so that blood could flow in from the healthy side of the heart; then they stitched him all back together with steel wire."

Marco was especially impressed with the saw, which might have reminded him of some horror movie, and he asked my father detailed questions about the surgery, disappointed each time by the clinical scientific explanation that my father provided.

"So, after all this time, we're finally starting to breathe easy again," my mother confided to Hans. And it was true: I had started to go out again almost every evening with the Volvo, alone, free, and happy, after enjoying a few hours of tranquility at home. In the afternoons, though, I studied hard for my final high school exams.

Hans found us in this laboriously constructed idyll—it was hard not to notice, and so he behaved accordingly, courteous to my father, gallant with my mother, affectionate with Marco and me.

It was instinctive for me to show him the pair of photographs that had come in the mail a few days before from Roccalba. One showed the construction yard, with Giorgio Bellusci and my grandmother in the foreground throwing eggs, coins, and salt into the foundations of the Fondaco del Fico, while a cement mixer filled them with cement. The other picture showed a labyrinth of pillars photographed from below, and in the middle, still intact, the wall of jagged stones; in the middle of that wall, you could see the brushstroke of green that continued to grow: the fig tree, or "*fico*," of the Fondaco.

"Here, down by the river, is where he wants to put the swimming pool," my mother broke in, resting her index finger on a section of the second photo that was still covered by luxuriant grape vines.

"Mamma came up with that idea a long time ago," I put in promptly, knowing full well that she expected me to say it.

Hans Heumann put on his eyeglasses to make out the

details. His face lit up. "*In gamba, Giorgio*," he said in Italian. Then he went on in German. "So he'll finally be able to make his dream come true! Even back then I knew he wouldn't let it go: he is a stubborn one. I understood it from his fiery eyes. I admire him and I love him. I'd like to see him again, in happier conditions than the last time."

Now Hans grew thoughtful. And silent. My father took advantage of the moment; he had been waiting impatiently ever since Hans arrived. As excited as a small boy with a good report card, he showed Hans a long article that had appeared in a *prestigious*—he lingered on the word—American magazine, and the other press clippings, carefully collected in an album, that spoke highly of the article.

He never should have done it.

Hans's voice and expression became a distillate of acid sarcasm. "Well, good for you," he said, "now you'll be famous! But, let me warn you, that American magazine is well known for its unreliability. Just think, once it dared to recommend that its readers invest in original prints of big-name photographers, and it printed a list that someone had thrown together of the top hundred photographers in the world, along with the commercial value of their work, as if they were listing prices for vegetables at a truck farm."

While my father was ruefully closing the magazine and his album, and my mother stood looking at Hans with undisguised scorn, I couldn't help but ask him where he had been placed in the list. "Certainly at the top, don't you think?" Hans replied, "but I'll tell you, I could never bring myself even to open that stupid magazine." And he burst into laughter; I was even more disappointed in him for that arrogant wisecrack than for his harsh baiting of my father.

It is incredible how devastating words can be. Was it possible that Hans didn't know it, or that he just didn't care? Now that he had tossed a bomb into the happy family setting, obliterating my parents' smiles and wounding my newfound admiration for him, there was nothing left for him to do but play with Marco or caress his young wife, as was his now well-established habit. Hélène had said little or nothing that evening, and seemed not to have understand her husband's cruel jokes, or to have noticed my parents' resentment. She smiled nonchalantly, a heartfelt smile, though just then there seemed to be no reason to smile. I looked at her: her beauty was spectacular, bursting with life and health, the kind of woman that would be described in Calabria, without restraint, as a "*bonazza*." In contrast with the elderly Hans, the embittered Klaus, and the furious Rosanna—three figures with faded, pale outlines—she filled her space like some majestic statue by Michelangelo, almost inviting you to touch her. I considered it for a moment, I have to confess; even though she was my grandfather's wife, and therefore, officially, my grandmother; even though at the time I was crazy about Martina, kissing her over the phone, yearning for the moment when I would finally be able to kiss her in the flesh, in early July, in Roccalba.

THIRD JOURNEY

I was arriving.

In my suitcase I carried my high-school diploma in case I decided to enroll in an Italian university. I had taken my final high-school exams at the end of May. The result of all those hours of studying had been a miserable grade that had disappointed my parents and, to some extent, me, too. But from that day forward, I felt relieved and I was ready for a well-deserved rest.

My mother was more relaxed that summer; she was blooming like the cherry tree in our backyard. It is just incredible, I thought to myself, the years go by, life poisons her blood, but in the end she is always renewed, as if time just tickled her as it passes. Her wrinkles, at age forty, are barely visible with a magnifying glass; her breasts are as firm as if she'd had silicone implants. Maybe it was her son, the other one, her youngest, just eight-and-a-half years old, who kept her young.

Anyway, I was feeling pretty relaxed myself. I had decided to take a year off (time to "do some thinking," as I said self-importantly in front of others), before starting college or looking for a job. I would spend the summer in Roccalba, with Martina.

The airplane was crowded with emigrants going back to Calabria for the summer holidays. When my mother took me to the airport in Hamburg, she sang to herself the whole time, the way she does when she's worried about something. Just before they called my flight, she hugged me tight to her, and whispered a broken phrase in my ear: "Listen, you be careful . . . "

At the time I didn't understand: she was afraid I would never come back.

The flight was long and boring. I listened to music on my Walkman, noticed a few clouds shaped like lambs, and thought to myself that if Hans Heumann had been there, he probably would have taken pictures of them. I thought about Giorgio Bellusci, too, but only in passing. In the end, I wasn't going to Roccalba to see him; I was going to see Martina. Or, at least, that's what I thought. Recently, she had been writing me two letters a week, and I had been calling her every two or three days. An unbroken stream of written and whispered words that did little to eliminate the distance separating us. I had to see her as soon as possible; we were both aching to be together. So I decided to move up my departure, without telling her. I wanted to surprise her. I thought of the young Klaus traveling to Roccalba, trying to imagine how Rosanna would react when she saw him. And in a sudden final fade, the scene was overlaid by the image of the girl that Al Pacino fell in love with. I had given my parents a videocassette of "The Godfather" and then watched it with them. I too was troubled and captivated—as my father had been when he was young— by that dark girl taking off her clothes, in silhouette, in the heat of a Mediterranean summer. A husky, emotional voice echoed my own voice, repeating: enough, that's enough, now it's time for you to leave, go, go to Roccalba, Martina is waiting for you. A second later, I turned to look at my father: his eyes were glistening, maybe just because of the hours he spent in front of a computer, and he was holding his Rosanna's hand. As they held hands, I could see a tiny, momentary tremor, perhaps an instant of regret crushed by the pressure of their hands. The next day I bought a plane ticket to Lamezia airport.

I thought about all this during the flight. But untroubled thoughts, as easy and calm as those about Martina, who was waiting for me in Roccalba.

Now the plane was flying over the Gulf of Sant'Eufemia and suddenly, in a sharp turn, the aircraft angled its nose down toward the airport, as if it were sick and tired of the turquoise water of the Tyrrhenian Sea.

If only I had a moment's foreshadowing of what would happen just a short time later, I would have jumped out of the plane and into those waves, without a parachute.

I was dying to embrace Martina again, with the same passion as Al Pacino, but she was still at the beach, in Tropea, with her sister's family; she hadn't expected me so soon: she couldn't be home for a week, any sooner would hurt her sister's feelings. She loved me so much, and sent me a kiss. That is what Teresa said, when she came to pick me up at the airport with her father's car. She hugged me and gave me Martina's kiss on the lips.

The Fiat Tempra zipped quickly along the stretch of super-highway until it reached Pizzo. Then it turned inland, climbing the road to Roccalba. The moist heat poured in through the open windows, cutting off my breathing. Luckily I was almost there. I looked straight ahead to keep from vomiting, and listened as Teresa talked.

The whole way, she told me the latest news about the construction work on the Fondaco del Fico, which was the main topic of conversation that summer in Roccalba, she said. All the emigrants who had come back for their summer holidays, women, men, and children, everyone, even the inhabitants of neighboring villages, cared passionately about it. Some were for it, others were against it, and they argued like fans of opposing soccer teams, shouting and cursing, cheering their side on, even ready to brawl about it. In any case, Grandpa Giorgio had surprised just about everyone, even his own relations, Teresa admitted. No one expected that after nearly eight years in prison, after a heart attack and major heart surgery, at his age, he would seriously start building a hotel. People admired him and criticized him. Young people would cluster around him, in the evenings at the bar, listening to his every word. Grandpa Giorgio was a character, and he knew how to tell stories. He talked about the past and the future, but he'd always come back to the Fondaco del Fico, with stories about travel and dreams that were better than any movie.

Teresa talked as she drove carefully, skillfully avoiding the worst potholes that still dotted the road, as they always had, in zigzag patterns the whole length of the route leading up to Roccalba. I looked down to my right, toward the Fondaco del Fico, but I couldn't see it. It was hidden by the tall Holm oaks that lined the road. Roccalba, on the other hand, was clearly visible high atop the hill, like a horseshoe with a white halo of light around it.

Finally, I was arriving.

Yes, Grandpa Giorgio was likable, and young people especially seemed to like him, Martina most of all, Teresa was saying. Some of the grownups, on the other hand, just thought he was crazy, and that prison had damaged his last remaining scraps of grey matter. Even her father, Uncle Bruno, thought he was crazy, unfortunately. Rebuilding the Fondaco del Fico in the middle of the country, far from Roccalba, and far from the beach, was just the sort of thing a stubborn conceited mule would do, Uncle Bruno said; it wasn't going to be a country inn, it would be a country shit-house, where travelers would stop to take a dump, out of the hot sun and the pouring rain, and then leave. Grandpa Giorgio really didn't seem to care what the others thought; he went his own way. He had already spent all his savings, he had sold his properties, where the old butcher shop had once been, and most of his land; he had even made my grandmother sell her father's old house in Bari and the little cottage in Camigliatello, which no one had used for decades. He wanted to do things in style. And Grandpa Giorgio was going to succeed.

We arrived in Roccalba late in the afternoon. I asked her to stop the car in the middle of the main square. I got out and, in a theatrical gesture, I knelt down to kiss the pavement of the village, partly in jest. I could feel the muggy heat bearing down on the back of my neck, but the porphyry tiles stretching out all around me, the tiles I wanted to kiss, were covered with white sparrow droppings, splattered out like a skyful of stars, while the guilty parties swooped and twittered in the lowering sky, madly mocking me or perhaps greeting me in their fashion. I finally had to give up, as Teresa laughed; in any case, whether it had been a joke or simply ridiculous, my intention to kiss the tiles clearly told me that Roccalba had a hold of me, and whether I liked it or not, it was a part of me, as much as Hamburg, no more and no less, and perhaps the mysterious voice that I had heard during "The Godfather" was the voice of Roccalba, calling me back to it, like a lover betrayed, using as bait a girl with a heaving breast who looked a lot like Martina.

At home, my grandmother and Aunt Elsa were waiting to greet me and fuss over me. As I hugged them, I could feel myself enveloped in the warmth of their abundant flesh. Aunt Elsa kept gaining weight; sooner or later she would equal my grandmother and, in turn, she would be equaled by Teresa. It was as if the three of them had been made from the same mold, just in different sizes; three Russian nesting dolls made of firm, healthy flesh. Giorgio Bellusci, of course, was at the Fondaco del Fico, my grandmother told me, supervising construction. He shouldn't tire himself out, but a little exercise was good for him; even the doctors said so.

Uncle Bruno was at the bar and, as soon as he heard I had arrived, he came to say hello. He had become as round as a little keg. He seemed shorter than the last time I had seen him. In reality, he was just wider, and I had grown taller.

"How are you?" I asked, and I had to look down as I spoke

to him, because the top of his head was shorter than my shoulder.

"Fine," he said cheerfully, "wonderful, doesn't it show?" And he pointed proudly to his belly. "I'm eating well and I'm screwing very well, the two finest things in life, what more could you ask?"

Aunt Elsa looked over at him in disgust; my grandmother and Teresa hadn't heard him, luckily; they were in the kitchen making dinner.

Later, when we sat down to dinner, I realized that at least as far as eating was concerned, Uncle Bruno hadn't been lying. He ate like a pig; and I mean, literally like a pig, with the same eager excitement, slurping, gnawing, smearing his snout in the food, belching. It was a sight to see, incredible to hear the sounds he emitted. Then Giorgio Bellusci came in, with a huge watermelon, a gift, he said, from a farmer. He set the watermelon down on the table, and said hello to me. Uncle Bruno began to eat like a human being again. It reminded me of the watermelon from that bloody summer, but I didn't mention that.

Giorgio Bellusci sat down and began to eat and talk; he asked about my mother, Marco, my father; he asked about Hans Heumann, and said that he would give anything to see him again. He spoke in his stubborn voice. The bypass operation had clearly rejuvenated him. He was more energetic than before. Then he started talking about the work on the Fondaco del Fico, but my eyes started to close, maybe because I was tired from the trip, or from the wine I had drunk. I managed to stay awake until Giorgio Bellusci split open the watermelon by resting the tip of the blade on the rind. He gave me the rooster's crest, and I gave half of it to Teresa. I ate it avidly and, immediately afterward, went to bed.

I slept until ten in the morning. Giorgio Bellusci was waiting for me at the Fondaco del Fico, my grandmother told me, as she brought me a cup of coffee and a slice of homemade almond cake in bed. As I was without a car, he had left his old one for me in the garage; I could use it to go to the beach or just to drive around. My grandfather had bought a brand-new pickup truck, which he needed to take building materials out to the Fondaco del Fico.

The car was the old iron-grey Simca, covered with dust inside and out. It finally started, on the sixth try, when I figured I had already flooded the engine. It farted repeatedly all the way up the steep climb to the main square, like an old mule carrying a heavy load, but all the way down the S-curves to the river it went fast, even too fast, because the brake pads were worn out. Whenever I tried to slow down it emitted a mournful trumpeting sound.

I parked in the broad dirt clearing, next to Giorgio Bellusci's pickup truck.

"Good morning, young man," he greeted me cheerfully. "How's the Ferrari running?"

"Well, she farts like a mule, and she complains like a she-elephant when you try to step on her sore old brakes, but otherwise, fine, just fine."

We both laughed happily. The construction workers laughed with us as they unloaded sacks of cement from a big red truck. They were from Roccalba, and they called out greetings to me as if we were all old friends.

Then Giorgio Bellusci nodded toward the building. My mother's stories and the photographs had all made me imagine the Fondaco del Fico as a small, cozy country house.

"Well, what do you think of it?" Giorgio Bellusci asked, tugging at my sleeve, since I had fallen silent.

"It's big," I said. "I didn't expect it to be so . . . imposing."

In front of me stood three stories held aloft by cement pillars and topped by a double-vaulted reinforced-concrete roof that truly was imposing; on the left, where the stables once stood, the roof projected like the prow of a ship, supported by small round columns.

"I could hardly rebuild it the way it used to be, just a tavern with a tiny kitchen, four little bedrooms upstairs, and a cellar for barrels and provisions! Times have changed. I decided to build fourteen guest rooms, a first-class restaurant, and a bar; I want it to have everything we'll need, including a swimming pool, like your mother suggested. A real hotel, not huge, but well equipped. To compete with all the other hotels around here."

Between the two central pillars stood the old stone wall, charred at the top. I asked Giorgio Bellusci why he hadn't knocked it down.

"You don't see? You're so smart, and you don't get it? We're going to leave it on display, in the middle of the new wall. And we're going to leave that little fig tree growing out of the stones, you see? Who can say, maybe it's a direct descendant of the fig tree that they named this inn after so many years ago. It will grow to be a tall tree; you'll see. Fig trees can grow in the cement; they'd grow on the moon if you planted one there."

One of the construction workers, maybe the contractor, butted in. "Go ahead and tell him, boy," he said, "the old wall doesn't work with a new building. It just looks wrong."

"I like it," I answered. "I think it's a good idea." And the bricklayer replied, "Well, yeah, what was I thinking? Same brood, after all!"

He smiled at me, and went calmly back to work.

Giorgio Bellusci brusquely liquidated the question: "Here everyone wants to be an architect, even the bricklayers, but they don't understand a fucking thing. They don't know what's beautiful or what's ugly. They know how to do things, but they lack imagination." Then he took me inside the structure and explained the plans in detail. He showed me the porcelain fixtures he had selected, the furnishings for the bedrooms, the brand of tiles that he would use for the pool. He seemed possessed, as if he were a saint performing a miracle or battling the devil. He showed me the plans for the cellar, too, and told me that when they dug on the site of the old root cellar, the remains of the brigands had emerged, along with a few charred fragments of rifles, gnawed away at by rats and mice and the passage of time. He had placed those heartbreaking remains in a coffin that the construction workers had made out of a few extra boards, and he had asked the parish priest to bless them, before taking them to the ossuary in the village cemetery, where they could finally rest in peace. After all, they were Christians too, concluded Giorgio Bellusci.

I would go down to the Fondaco del Fico once or twice every day: I brought cold beers for the construction workers, I spent time with Giorgio Bellusci, keeping him company, and I helped out on some of the work. In town, without Martina, I was bored, especially during the day. And I got bored on the beach, the one time I went down without her.

Giorgio Bellusci was grateful. "At last, I can talk to someone with a brain," he said to me. He talked to the construction workers in a hostile tone of voice; before or after some piece of work, quarrels would erupt that often threatened to degenerate into genuine fistfights at any minute; instead, they always ended with a conciliatory round of beers. "Well, you're the one who's paying," the contractor would say, rubbing thumb and forefinger together. And, sometimes, when Giorgio Bellusci turned his back, he would tap his forefinger against his temple.

When Martina came back from Tropea, she couldn't find me in town, so she asked Teresa to drive her out to the Fondaco del Fico. She was tanned and rested, but she looked nothing like the dark girl that Al Pacino married. And why should she? Martina was Martina, and I was just a fool who had let a movie fill his head with ideas.

We kissed, briefly, not the way we both wanted to. The construction yard was full of curious eyes, and it wasn't the right time for public displays of affection. Giorgio Bellusci was very nice to her: he asked after her father and her emigrant sister, he offered her a cold beer, he showed her the plans for the hotel, and he even opened the front door of the Simca for her: "Prego, lovely *signorina*, take a seat." He had understood that Martina would be leaving with me. He gave Teresa a kiss, and slapped me on the back of the neck, saying loudly: "Ah, Florian, how I envy you! Oh, how I envy you, darling boy. Now, take my advice . . . eh! Otherwise, you'll regret it when you're old!"

We drove off, followed by Teresa and a flock of swallows. Teresa overtook us on the first straight stretch of road. A short distance later, we turned off onto a dirt lane and I parked the car in the shade of a large elderberry bush. We were finally alone. I would have preferred to make love outside, in the open air; but it was better to be cautious about the apparent solitude of the location, and there could be vipers lying in ambush under the dry grass; Martina was terrified of snakes. It was hot inside the car; I opened all the windows. Along with the pungent scent of elderberry there came the overwhelming sound of crickets chirping and swallows chattering.

Our first kiss was an endless draft of sweet wine. I felt giddy, half tipsy. Big as I am, I felt clumsy in the tiny Simca; I tore buttons off her blouse and I couldn't get her bra unhooked. "I love you, Martina, I love you," I said over and over, in an obvious but necessary singsong. I was sweating; she wasn't; she undressed calmly, and when I saw brown areolas of her breasts, in close-up, just in front of my mouth, and felt the tight warm curls of her crotch brushing against me, I came close to fainting.

For the rest of that August, the Simca was our bed, because the real bed, the big soft one, was temporarily being used by its rightful owner, Martina's sister.

Occasionally, I would run the risk of taking Martina to the beach, over in the area around Soverato, on the Ionian Sea. I'd had the Simca's brakes replaced, but the mechanic warned me that if I wanted to drive the car without worries, I needed to have the engine rebuilt entirely. We stayed on the beach until late, and at night we'd go get something to eat in a pizzeria and then come back to the beach, embracing on the warm sand until midnight, even later. Sometimes, we'd take Teresa with us. Not only was she Martina's best friend and my cousin, she was our cover—she tried to protect us from the indiscreet eyes of other people and from vicious gossip. Moreover, she could lie even better than I could, and I was a very good liar. She told my folks and Martina's parents that we were going dancing, or to some pop concert. Only rarely was that true. In other words, she would cover our tracks and sometimes she'd actually be our lookout, that is, when she wasn't lying on the warm sand with whomever she was dating at the time, or in the car with him. Teresa had a right to her own bit of fun, after all.

In town, we would stroll along the Corso together, Teresa

arm in arm with Martina, while I walked with the cluster of their assorted friends, who were formidable chatterers. And formidably touchy. They would tell me all of the most blood-thirsty stories about their village, with the twists and turns of the paybacks and vendettas and the endless succession of trials that ensued. The law student and soon-to-be lawyer Arcuri considered himself quite an expert on this subject. If, howev-er, I dared to take the bait and say, you know, you're right, it must be tough to live in Roccalba, they immediately took offense, and shot back that you couldn't dream of finding a vil-lage as nice as Roccalba anywhere in Germany. Then they'd move on to the subject of soccer: the Italian national team was far superior to the German team, they'd say. They could never make me mad, though, no matter how hard they tried. All I cared about was Martina; I'd watch out of the corner of my eye her nervous gait, certain that she was thinking only about me.

Once we were outside of the village, I would break off from the cluster of young people and catch up with her. Usually the group stopped at the soccer field to watch the match, while the two of us would continue on to the park in the grove of Holm oaks. Our goldfish were waiting for us; they were much liveli-er than in winter; much happier; in particular, they were better fed because many tourists and entire emigrant families on vacation would picnic around the little lake and then toss scraps of bread and other leftovers into the water.

In early September, though, life turned dull again, even for the goldfish. There was no one to cheer them up; we were the only ones bringing them bits of bread and the occasional worm that Martina managed to steal from her father. The village had emptied out; hundreds of cars and entire families had driven north, returning to cities in northern Italy and northern Europe. The sky too would soon be emptying out, as Giorgio Bellusci pointed out to me one day; the swallows seemed to be going crazy. It meant that they were preparing for their long southward journey. "Ah, the swallows, the swallows, we should really erect a monument to the swallows; if it weren't for them, flies and mosquitoes would eat us alive. I hope that next year, by the time they return, the Fondaco del Fico will be ready for them to nest in."

Giorgio Bellusci was satisfied with the way things were going. Work was proceeding nicely; there were no surprises in terms of timing or costs. The money that he had received for the sale of his buildings and farmland would suffice. He was proud that he hadn't had to borrow anything, not a single lira. At dinner every evening he was cheerful, and was even courteous to Uncle Bruno, when we all ate together. After watching the evening news on TV, he'd go to bed, because he woke up every morning at four-thirty; I, on the other hand, would go to the bar, like all the other kids my age in town. In those few months I had become one of them—I talked loudly, I had the same wavy hair, now turned dark once and for all. I stood out for my height, but that was true in Hamburg as well.

At ten-thirty on the dot I had my nightly date with Martina. I left the bar and headed toward her sister's house; the sister had left some time ago. I knocked softly on the door. I heard a cautious: "Is that you?" and I answered: "It's me, my love."

In bed, exploring the length and breadth of her body with my lips, like an experienced, tireless traveler, I learned that Martina was much more beautiful than Al Pacino's dark girlfriend, warmer and more deeply in love.

I was in bed with Martina, at her sister's house, that night. It must have been around eleven-thirty. We were talking quietly, as always, for fear that someone might hear us from the road. A prolonged, muted roar filled the room, like the echoing report of a distant avalanche. Instinctively, Martina held me tighter. We were naked beneath the sheets.

"It was just thunder," I reassured her. "It'll start raining hard soon." It was October and it was drizzling out. "Maybe we'd better head home, before it really starts pouring down," I added, and she agreed.

A hum of voices rose from the street; they sounded increasingly excited, and we finally started to worry. "Do you think it was an earthquake?" Martina asked. I tried to calm her down again with a last long kiss of farewell. It did no good. She was trembling. We dressed and slipped out, quietly, each heading in a different direction. In the main square, there were lots of people, and they were worried. "It sounded to me like a big fireworks display." "No, it was definitely an earthquake." "No, that's not it. It must have been a landslide. The side of the mountain must have come down." "No, you're wrong. The noise came from down in the plain."

"It was an explosion," an old man finally said. "Dynamite, I'm positive. It came from down there, somewhere around the riverbed."

I saw Giorgio Bellusci's pickup truck come barreling along at top speed. I waved to him to stop and I got in. By now, I had guessed what had happened, but I hoped I was wrong; I didn't say a thing to Giorgio Bellusci, and he said nothing to me. He was focused on driving; he honked as he tore through the curves, taking them the way an ambulance would.

When we got down onto the flatlands, we could smell blasting powder. It was clear now: someone had blown up the Fondaco del Fico.

I'll never forget his animal scream in the dark of the night, when the pickup truck's headlights swung around to illuminate the mound of reinforced concrete, still shrouded in a slowly settling cloud of dust. There it was, the murderous fury, something I never could have imagined in my wildest dreams.

"Sons of bitches bastards, I'll snap your necks with my hands; you're destroying my life; I'll shove that dynamite right up your assholes, I'll crush your worthless souls, you're destroying this land of ours. You won't go to hell, you'll go nowhere, you'll disappear for all time, from this world and the next!"

I didn't dare try to calm him down. What could I have done? He was kicking at the earth like a madman; he threw rocks at all that remained of the building, as if he were stoning a hated phantom.

The Fondaco del Fico was a shapeless heap of rubble, a sand castle dashed to earth by angry children.

After about a half hour, he calmed down on his own; he climbed back into the pickup truck and I followed him, looking at the ground. There was a darkness in my head that weighed me down.

Back home, everyone was awake, my grandmother, my uncle and aunt, Teresa. "Well?" asked Uncle Bruno.

Giorgio Bellusci answered: "I'm tired; I'm going to bed; good night."

So I had to describe the rubble to them; I had to comfort my weeping grandmother and aunt, while my uncle said over and over in an exhausted monotone: "I knew this would hap-

pen sooner or later; everyone knew it; those people don't forgive and they don't forget."

I finally went to sleep after hours and hours of wakefulness.
As I walked by Giorgio Bellusci's big bedroom, I heard him
snore heavily, as always. And, as always, he woke up at four-
thirty on the dot, made a pot of coffee, and left the house to go
to the ruins of the Fondaco del Fico.

And so, once again, it was my job to explain what I had seen
to the crowd of people clustering in front of the house early the
next morning. They stood there sadly, they listened to my story
and did their best to console us, they reached out to shake
hands in a sign of solidarity, at least in their intentions; because
really they seemed like a crowd of people who had just attend-
ed a funeral and were now politely conveying their condolences to the family of the victim. The Fondaco del Fico was
dead; it had been murdered. Amen.

Condolences continued to pour in for days, especially at
night, when Giorgio Bellusci came home. There were phone
calls as well, from Italy and other countries. In the end, our visitors knew how it had all happened even better than we did.
They had attached explosives to the central pillars, and someone had hidden in the woods and detonated the explosives
from there. It had been a professional job. Only the side structure, the section of roof that looked like the prow of a ship, still
stood, almost intact. All the rest of the structure lay broken,
covered with dust.

The carabinieri were following various leads, people said,
repeating what they read in the newspapers. Around here, this
sort of thing belonged to the past. The carabinieri couldn't
understand it, and Giorgio Bellusci was offering no help.

"Do you suspect anyone?" they had asked him.

And he said: "Everyone on earth."

And they said: "This is no time for jokes, Signor Bellusci."

And he said: "Then don't bust my balls with these stupid questions."

The soon-to-be lawyer Arcuri, however, said he understood: "It's obvious, and it was predictable. It's a warning, marked 'to whom it may concern.' A symbolic act, meaning: don't kid yourselves, you can kill one of us, even arrest some of us, but you won't get away with it. We own the territory, we do with it as we please, whenever we choose." It was chilly in the square that evening, and he was talking excitedly, heatedly, to me, Martina, and a couple of friends, as if he were addressing the court. In any case, he, Arcuri, would not have been at all surprised if, instead of blowing up the Fondaco del Fico, they had blown up Giorgio Bellusci himself, guilty of an affront unlike anything the village and surrounding area had seen in human memory. Perhaps it was a sign that times were changing. "Well, it's better this way," Martina broke in, to console me, "better that an unfinished building should be destroyed by a bomb, rather than a man. And a good man, too."

What neither Arcuri, nor Martina, nor the people that came to pay their condolences, nor my grandmother, nor my other relations—what nobody could have dreamed was that Giorgio Bellusci, a few days after the explosion, would roll up his sleeves and start working again.

It wasn't easy for him. Everyone told him to give up. "It's not worth it, Poppa," my mother told him over the phone. "You're old now, what do you care! Let us live in peace for the last few years that remain to us," my grandmother begged him, and relatives and neighbors and everyone else echoed her. But he was grim and determined.

He wouldn't give up even when the contractors in Roccalba refused to rebuild, offering feeble excuses: "We're too busy with other jobs."

He contacted builders in other towns, and they gave him estimates higher than the first one, considering the risks.

With the money that remained, he could barely afford to clear away the rubble and rebuild the foundations of the building that had been destroyed. He rebuilt the original piece of wall with his own hands, asking me to hunt around for all the old pieces of light-blue stone, one by one.

I was glad to help him. I liked his determination, his iron will, I liked his sense of pride. And I liked the way the family closed ranks around him: my parents and my uncle and aunt financed the reinforced concrete structure; in just a few weeks it was as solid and imposing as before.

Then Giorgio Bellusci started going from one bank to the next, trying to obtain financing, but he only managed to raise a few million lire—the value of the mortgage on his old house in town. He used that money to shore up the external pillars with bricks known as *ventunoforini* and some of the internal support pillars on the ground floor.

For the first time since the day of the explosion, he was clearly distraught: "I can't leave it like this, an abortion of a hotel; I'd be ashamed," he repeated over and over. He couldn't resign himself to failure. Anyway, he stood guard over the new construction; he often spent the night there, in a sleeping bag with a rifle.

"It's an unnecessary precaution," Arcuri said. "He can rest easy. They wanted to show who's boss, and they've done it."

Two days before Christmas, my parents and Marco arrived. They would only be staying in Roccalba for a week, because my father had a lot of work to do, but in the meantime they seemed happy as could be, and they kept saying how well we all looked, that I had gained weight and the grandparents looked years younger. I couldn't tell whether my parents were putting on an act to boost our morale, or if they just couldn't see what was written in our eyes. What I did understand was Marco's impatience; five minutes after they arrived, he said: "I'm going with my friends to find firewood for the Christmas Eve bonfire." And he left the house without asking permission.

When Marco came in from his tour around the village, dirty and dripping with sweat, Giorgio Bellusci hugged him tight and whispered in his ear. Marco threw his arms in the air in a sign of victory, and kissed his grandfather on the forehead, but he said nothing.

The next day was Christmas Eve. Early in the morning, Giorgio Bellusci woke Marco and me and drove us out to the Fondaco del Fico in his pickup truck. I understood as soon as I saw the chainsaw on the loading deck.

We worked half the day to cut oak branches, and Holm oak and mulberry stumps that had already been ripped out of the earth and piled up by the bulldozer in the woods behind the Fondaco del Fico. A cold, dank wind was blowing, and gusts of rain fell from time to time, but we toiled away without complaining. At last, we loaded all the wood onto the pickup truck, and took it to the square in front of the church, carefully piling it on top of the logs and branches that the village children had already gathered. "The Christ Child will be happy," Giorgio Bellusci said to us, as we stood admiring the mountain of firewood. "So will I, very," Marco added seriously.

We were starving by the time we got home, and we found my mother, my aunt, and Teresa helping my grandmother to make the traditional thirteen-course Christmas Eve dinner. Finally, we started to breathe the air of the holidays.

Late that evening, in front of the church, I saw my mother holding tight to Giorgio Bellusci, clearly profoundly moved as she stood watching the Christmas Eve bonfire; Marco in the meanwhile was explaining to our father that there had never been such a big bonfire in Roccalba, not even in the time of Focubellu—even Grandpa said so.

Martina was standing on the church steps, and she waved to me to come over. As I walked behind Giorgio Bellusci, I heard him saying again to my mother: "The Christ Child will be happy, tonight. And so will Marco."

During that holiday season it seemed as if Giorgio Bellusci had forgotten all his problems. If he looked gloomy, as soon as he laid eyes on Marco, a smile came to his face. The two of them would often go out together to play cards in various bars. When lunch or dinnertime rolled around, they returned home to enjoy, with the rest of the family, my grandmother's flavorful cooking and the grapes, melons, and pomegranates that Giorgio Bellusci kept in his cool cellar.

None of us mentioned the Fondaco del Fico, not even my mother, or my aunt and uncle, perhaps out of fear of spoiling Christmas.

My father finally violated that tacit accord: he asked for an update on how work was going on the Fondaco del Fico, and suggested a way to get a little money. We were driving in the car, and my mother and Marco were in the back seat. I was driving them to the airport of Lamezia for their flight home. To me, the method that my father suggested seemed cruel, but necessary. My mother, however, immediately began screaming at him: "Did I hear you right? You must have your brains in your feet! A fine idea you come up with! An idea that I would expect only from a certified turd!" They fought the whole rest of the way to the airport. My mother wouldn't speak to him until they boarded, and, for all I know, for the rest of the flight. As they said goodbye to me, they all cried out in chorus: "*Komm bald nach, wir warten auf dich. Ti aspettiamo. A presto.*"

I thought about my father's idea for a long time. It wasn't the suggestion of a "certified turd," at all. It was a good idea. But I didn't know how to suggest it to Giorgio Bellusci. And how would he react? Would he spit in my eye? Or grab me in a bear hug of joy?

I finally mustered the courage to speak to him. We were at the Fondaco del Fico, the two of us, alone, leaning our backs against that abortion of a hotel.

I said: "In Rome, there is an auction house called Christie's Italia; they sell all sorts of antiques, including manuscripts. If something has real value, they pay good money. My father says that we could get at least twenty million lire for Dumas's album. He checked into it."

How did Giorgio Bellusci respond? He looked at me, incredulous and furious, and then he answered, in an angry, broken voice: "You. . . how could you. . . then . . . you never understood. . . a thing! If anyone else had said that to me . . . I would have smashed his face."

I walked away without another word, climbed into the Simca, and drove off, burning rubber as I left. Still, I couldn't be mad at him, I couldn't hold a grudge against that man that I saw in the rear-view mirror, stiff with discouragement, his eyes clenched in a squint of pain, his back to the wall, as if he were waiting to be executed by a firing squad.

That evening I felt like going back to Hamburg. "I can't stay here, in this sea of shit," I said bluntly to Martina. We were walking together along the Corso. Martina thought I was kidding, and she replied in jest: "Hey, watch how you talk, potato-eater." I took her in my arms and embraced her in the middle of the street. "I'm not joking; I'm going back to Hamburg. This has nothing to do with you."

"What's the matter, Florian, what's wrong with you? I've never seen you so blue."

What was the matter? Not even I knew what was wrong. I remained mute. There was a knot of anguish that was throttling me. "What's wrong, Florian? Talk to me." I had a darkness in my head that had been coming and going as it pleased since the day of the explosion, and I couldn't think straight. I started at the end, from the argument I had had with Giorgio Bellusci that afternoon. I told her about my father's sensible idea; I told her how mad I was at Giorgio Bellusci, as if his rejection had wounded me mortally. I said, in my fury: "That man is insane, I'm not going to stick with him anymore."

I never should have said it. Martina puffed out her cheeks, red as a pair of hot peppers, and then flew into a rage: "You're just a big baby, that's all, a baby with a chip on his shoulder. *Zu Giorgio* is right not to want to sell the Dumas manuscript. For him, it would be like selling a piece of his heart. And I thought that you were like him! You don't understand that man even a little bit. He does what he says, he's a serious man, not like the rest of the people in this village, who can't do anything but say they're going to do this, and do that, and then they do nothing at all, they take no risks, they only criticize people who try to do something, who try to take a step forward, who try to open a breach, try to see the light, create a future. We can't abandon him now, not now, especially not you, you're his nephew, you can't close your eyes, you can't run home to your mamma. *Zu Giorgio* needs your help now..."

I interrupted. I couldn't stand to listen anymore. "Is that right? Since you're so smart and know everything, why don't you tell me what I should do to help him?"

"If you're talking about money, there is only one way to get it . . . "

"I know, rob a bank . . . "

"Idiot! I'm not talking to you anymore tonight, you don't care a thing about me and what I say. Good-bye." And she walked off toward the lane that led to her house.

The darkness in my mind was total.

The next morning she came to my grandparents' house to see me. I was having breakfast in the kitchen. She greeted me with a kiss on the cheek. She was calm and smiling. She looked me straight in the eye and asked if she could talk to me without being interrupted by stupid wisecracks. I hadn't slept all night long; I was more tired and confused than before. I asked her if she wanted some coffee. Then I said: "I'm listening." And Martina proceeded to explain how to get the money; the simplest way, maybe, she said, the only way.

I felt my cheeks wrinkle into a long, amazed smile. "You're right, we could try," I told her. "Let's not say anything to anybody, yet. If we say anything, it'll be a huge disappointment." And I gave her a clumsy, misplaced kiss, between her upper lip and her nose.

I wasted no time; I immediately placed three or four international calls, and I managed to make an appointment in Lugano.

At lunch I told my grandparents that I was going away for a few days, to see friends in Rome.

*

Giorgio Bellusci walked into my bedroom without knocking. I was packing my bag to return home. He said that he wanted to talk to me. He was holding the wooden box that contained his treasures, and his dream that had been blown sky-high. He opened the box and carefully removed Dumas's Album. The room was suddenly filled with the startling scent of bergamot.

"I've given a lot of thought to your idea. I apologize for my bullheaded reaction. Dumas would have been happy to be helpful at this difficult time. And things like this become even more precious if they are useful to the present, or maybe I should say, to the future. I am entrusting you with our manuscript. And thank your father for the suggestion."

He hugged me. It was the first time he had ever hugged me. He was finally letting his Dumas go, and he wanted to comfort himself with the warmth of someone who loved him. He too smelled of bergamot.

I took the evening train for Lugano. I would stop in Rome on my way back. I held Dumas's album clamped under my arm for fear it might be stolen. I laid it under the pillow in sleeping compartment, and fell asleep with the intoxicating aroma of bergamot in my nostrils.

"Giorgio's smart, but he's unlucky," Hans Heumann said in Italian as soon as I finished explaining why I was there. I was sitting across from him and his wife Hélène, in the lobby of a hotel overlooking Lake Lugano. Then he went on in German: "I noticed it immediately; a little crazy, but smart. How many years has it been since we first met? (Oh, my Lord, I'd better not say, or Hélène will be sorry she married me.) He had gotten himself lost, so he was running along with both eyes closed; think of that! I was approaching a grade, and first I saw a red dog come over the top of the hill, followed by him. I came very close to running him over with my Käfer. Literally a fraction of a second. What saved his life was that I put on the brakes when I saw the dog. I was furious with him, I really swore at him, but in German. The dog was wagging its shaggy tail. It had saved his life. Giorgio looked at me as if he had just awoken from a deep sleep. His eyes were a color I had never seen before—a sunburnt brown. I offered him a ride, and the dog got in the car with him. We stopped to eat at the first trattoria we came across, and I asked him if he wanted to work as my guide. Actually, I was more interested in using him as a model, his eyes had that special color. It was all there in his eyes: pride, tenderness, stubbornness, passion, fire, sun, and, in the center of the pupils, remnants of rain and rancor, just ready to burst forth. Yes, I know, I talk about him as if I were in love with him. And, I guess I was a little bit. Often, we fall in love with our opposites. I was running away; it's true, I was escaping a life without flavor. I worked for the city government, I was seeing a married woman who basically used me as her vibrator; I don't know if you can understand that. He was trying to go see a girl whom he had barely met; he admitted to me that he had never kissed her. When he found her, he was going to ask her to marry him. He knew what he wanted—he knew exactly what he wanted. He was only temporarily lost. I felt as if I had been lost my whole life. We traveled everywhere in Calabria; I took him to Bari, and the dog was with us the whole time. I was taking pictures with a new eye—neither entirely distanced, nor with a total attachment to my subject, the way so many photographers work. I was taking pictures now, if you can say this, with an eye suspended in midair. Him and his world. One evening he asked me to stop the Käfer along a country road, and he took me to see an old stone wall in a maze of thorn bushes, hedges, and fruit trees. This is the Fondaco del Fico, he said; you have to take a picture of this. Then he confided his dream to me: one day, he would bring the Fondaco del Fico back to life. The sky was tinged with a delicate light, the countryside was yellow and dark green, the muggy heat hit you like a good strong wine, and the swallows flew around and around over the Fondaco del Fico, never landing. They chattered and sang, but they produced a uniform, grieving sound, the best soundtrack imaginable for that breathless atmosphere in which I found myself suspended. Giorgio was silent, now, and he was an unconscious protagonist of a dream that struck me as familiar; a dream that I had dreamed—who can say when? Around evening we got to his village. I'll never forget the welcome we got, and not just from Giorgio and his family, but from all of Roccalba. Just think, the young people let me take part in their serenades. Oh, how we drank, the wine and the prosciutto and the cheeses, oh, to be back there again!"

I thought Hans Heumann's eyes were going to start tearing

up. He was deeply moved. He squeezed Hélène's hand to give himself strength. I, on the other hand, felt only impatience; why didn't Hans make up his mind, give me the answer I was sitting there waiting for? I'd told him all the details: how far work had progressed on the Fondaco del Fico, the explosion, Giorgio Bellusci's stubborn determination, how work had resumed, the lack of money, the rejections from the banks . . . Then I'd showed him Dumas's album and told him that we had decided to sell it at Christie's Italia, in Rome.

Hans Heumann sat silently and looked at me, lost in thought; Hélène had understood very little, because we spoke in German. Now, I thought to myself, he's going to ask me: what does that have to do with me? Throughout the journey, I had imagined this answer to ward it off; it would have meant the end of everything.

Finally Hans opened his mouth and spoke.

"I came back to Hamburg full of energy; I was focused on one thing only: developing the rolls of film; I had a whole travel bag filled with rolls of film. I worked day and night for two weeks. I printed hundreds of pictures. Then I made a final cut of about twenty shots. Before doing anything else, I quit my job and told that married woman, who had started bothering me again, to go to hell. I had decided to become a photographer. A professional photographer; that was my dream. Not for the money, believe me, but because I wanted to be a free man, free to travel, to lose myself, and even to find a new me, a different me. So I went to a photo agency that was famous in those years, Der Fotograf, I presented my photographs, and the director of the agency, who had sent me packing the year before with the usual pat phrases of dismissal, you know: these are nice pictures, but . . . said to me, with conviction: You've got more talent than you need, young man. We can definitely place these photographs in a major magazine.

"Just then a skinny girl came into the room; her small face

was hidden behind long blond hair. She worked in the photo agency; I remembered her vaguely. She looked at the pictures and then at me; at me and then at the pictures. Finally she left without saying a word.

"That evening, I waited for her outside the agency, and asked her out to dinner. She said no. I asked for her phone number and address. All I could get out of her was her name: Erika. The next day, I was back at the corner outside the Der Fotograf agency, with a beautiful bouquet of roses. Three months later we were married. The pictures were published in an American magazine. The closeup of Giorgio with long hair, the happy dog at his feet, was acclaimed by the leading critics of the time. Giorgio was looking proudly at the old wall of the Fondaco del Fico; overhead you could see dozens of swallows flying. Without realizing it, I had photographed a dream.

"Robert Capa himself wrote me to say that I had captured a dream: a dream, he emphasized, that he couldn't decipher, which was why he liked that picture so much. He wanted to meet me. Robert Capa, the great photographer, one of my idols, wrote that he wanted to meet Hans Heumann, mister nobody. Sadly, though, it never happened. Life is filled with missed opportunities. Just a few months later, at the age of forty-one, Robert Capa was blown up by a landmine, in Indochina. The same day I opened my first show in Hamburg. It was the end of May, 1954."

Hans Heumann paused, and I saw him drain a glass of red wine to the last drop. "If I understand you," he said, "you need my help."

"That's right. This is my idea; Giorgio Bellusci knows nothing about it."

He said: "It seems a pity that you want to sell the Dumas manuscript. I wouldn't do it, it really seems a pity. But tell me, how much money do you need?" he finally asked, and so the answer was yes, it was yes, I wanted to shout, thank you, thank you, instead, I tried to think, I had no idea how much money we needed. I took a guess: "For the moment, I think fifty million lire would be enough, I think."

Hans Heumann took out his checkbook and started writing. "I don't think that's enough," he said. "Anyway, tell Giorgio to call me when this money runs out. We'll find a solution, with all the people I know. I'm happy to be able to help you." He handed me the check.

I couldn't believe my eyes. It was a check for a hundred million lire. I understood that, as my mother claimed, Hans Heumann had plenty of money, but that sort of unstinting generosity, without even asking for collateral, and his willingness to help us in the future, left me bewildered. I would gladly have kissed his hands, his feet, I wanted to hug him. But I didn't. Instead, as I slid the check into my wallet, I said: "Thanks, we'll pay back every last penny." I didn't even notice that for the first time, I had used the plural, "we."

Hans Heumann read the gratitude in my voice, but especially in my eyes. I was deeply moved. He continued to talk as if Giorgio Bellusci and I were partners.

"Well, first of all, try to finish building the Fondaco del Fico; and listen carefully—keep me posted on everything. For today, you are our guest. You'll have to stand the boredom of a gallery opening; it's a personal show of mine, called 'Skies of the World,' but then the evening will be for the three of us, right Hélène?" he said, in English, "and we'll have time to talk."

At last, Hélène felt that she was involved. "It's wonderful," she said. She truly seemed to be happy to see me again. And she asked curiously what the leather-bound book was; it seemed to come from a hairdresser's waiting room, the way it smelled. Once I told her that it was a manuscript by Dumas and that I wanted to sell it, she said: "If you'll trust me and leave it here, I know who to talk to; I can get you the best price."

"Where?" I asked.

"Paris, of course."

Obviously, I couldn't say no, but I must have seemed reluctant. "Trust her," Hans Heumann told me. "Hélène knows what she's doing. She has an instinct for business."

I let go of the album as if I was handing over an old friend I'd never see again. I had a knot in my throat, but I managed to smile.

When I got out of the train at the station of Vibo Valentia, Martina was waiting for me. "Mission accomplished," I shouted across the distance that separated us. "I have the treasure in my wallet."

I was beaming. Martina praised me: "Good work!" I lifted her into the air and ran toward the parking lot, with Martina laughing on my shoulder.

Back home, I waved the check under the eyes of my grandmother and my uncle and aunt: a hard-won war trophy. I told them that Dumas's album was in good hands and, most important of all, that we could rely on Hans Heumann in the future as well. They treated me like a hero; they said so, too, with gleeful exaggeration: "You're the savior of the fatherland." They cheered for me and drank toasts to my health and Martina's (it had been her idea), Hélène's, and especially Hans Heumann's.

Giorgio Bellusci said only: "Thank you. I knew that I could count on you. The hog is ours, now!"

He didn't seem as euphoric as I had imagined. It was as if he expected this happy ending. Still, his facial muscles relaxed suddenly, and quite visibly, and I thought I could detect the beginnings of a smile of a relief.

The following day, I drove him to Catanzaro, where we deposited the check to his checking account. On the way back, we stopped in various construction outlets, placing orders for large quantities of bricks, cement, whitewash, and terracotta roof tiles. Giorgio Bellusci wanted to be sure that the roof tiles were the traditional kind, Siena earthenware, where the swallows would have no trouble building their nests, he said, just like in the roof of the old Fondaco del Fico.

From that day on, I worked full-time with Giorgio Bellusci: if necessary, I worked as a laborer, I took him shopping, I was at the Fondaco del Fico whenever the engineer who was overseeing construction came by; we worked together to solve technical problems that hadn't been in the plans.

With the engineer's help, we even found space for a sun room overlooking the sea. It had been Martina's idea, based on the hotel in Tropea where she had stayed with her sister.

"Do we need it?" Giorgio Bellusci asked me.

"Martina says we do," I answered him.

"Well, then, since we've done thirty, we'll make a stretch and do thirty-one, and that's all I have to say on the matter." On the last word, he clapped his hands: a sharp report that echoed through the countryside like a rifle shot. Giorgio Bellusci fell silent, as did the jaybirds. He pulled a bottle of wine out of his rucksack and took a long pull. "At last!" he said. His white hair tossed in the gusts of wind that blew off the two seas and crossed paths directly over the Fondaco del Fico. The jaybirds began to chatter again, and he spoke to me: "If I am reborn, I'll redo everything that I've ever done in my life. But I'll never kill a man again, not even a criminal like that one. It wasn't temporary insanity, like my lawyer claimed. Or maybe it was temporary insanity that lasted for a whole week. I sharpened that meat hook the day they burned the door of my butcher shop.

"And then, when I saw the sheep and the dogs hanging on the fence, I was sure of what I would do. I knew that they wouldn't stop, but I knew that I wouldn't stop either. A conceited donkey, that's what I was. I'll have blood on my hands forever. For no good reason. If you're alone, they crush your balls and make you dance like a monkey. Any move you make is the wrong move, when you're alone. For almost eight years, I was a dead man, but the worm was alive inside me, and it was devouring me all the same. I thought to myself: it was all pointless, a life spent rebuilding nothing, I'm a failure, a tree that bears no fruit, I've just piled rubble on the rubble I inherited, and nothing more. I missed the Fondaco del Fico as much as I missed my family."

Giorgio Bellusci walked toward the pickup truck. He moved as if he was tired and lost in thought, as if he regretted making that confession.

When we got home, we found a money order for twenty million lire. In the space for sender's comments was written: "The album is in good and appreciative hands. Best of luck! Hélène."

I felt useful; in fact, I felt indispensable; and even Giorgio Bellusci admitted I was, at dinner, in the presence of my grandmother and, whenever they were there, of my aunt and uncle, and Teresa. So for the moment I had abandoned the idea of going back to Hamburg, as my parents and Marco kept calling and asking me to. "I'll be back when everything's ready," I answered them.

"When?" my parents asked.

"After the summer, I think."

"Aren't you bored in Roccalba? This time of year, it's a morgue," my mother insisted, remembering the tedium of the springtimes of her youth.

I wasn't bored, I didn't have time to be bored. After an autumn and a winter of worries, the springtime had awakened me, along with nature at large.

Martina was right: "The nicest season, at least here in Roccalba, is springtime." We were in the park on the village outskirts. The air was warm and scented. Along the broad dirt road hawthorn flowers glittered, crowded with butterflies, and down below, the steep slopes were a festival of daisies, wild roses, purple rockrose, and elderberry bushes loaded down with flowers that opened out like umbrellas, marking the edges of the Holm oak forest, stained with thorny broom plants. You could hear the songs of dozens of birds hidden high in the foliage and the noisy darting flight of the first swallows in the sky.

We hadn't forgotten our little goldfish: the lake water was so clear that we could see their tiny round mouths opening to suck down—in the blink of an eye—the chunks of bread that we tossed them. Martina was leaning against the wooden fence that surrounded the little lake, talking to the fish; behind her, I was leaning against her back. I don't even know if she meant to do it but, without interrupting her one-sided conversation with the goldfish, she repeatedly rubbed her round ass against me, just below my navel. As she sensed my growing excitement, she twisted her neck around as far as she could, straining to reach my mouth with her tongue. My hands darted beneath her clothing, found her breasts, and seized them hungrily. Now our bodies fit together perfectly, and as she began to sway rhythmically, I followed the motion willingly. She was smooth and firm as a stone from the river. A hot, sun-baked stone. I pulled away in the nick of time. A spurting rainbow of white drops hurtled into the lake water, startling the goldfish.

"You're right," I said to her. "Springtime in Roccalba is beautiful."

My grandmother made a prediction based on the color of the sea; in early June, the water turned a dark violet. It was going to be a long, hot summer.

We were leaning our elbows on the railing of her balcony, almost overflowing with red, white, and variegated chrysanthemums. In the distance we could see the dark-brown roof tiles of the Fondaco del Fico; around the building the plain stretched out in the sunlight like a straw-yellow flower. In the further distance, the dark purple of the Tyrrhenian Sea was tinged with stripes of indigo and azure; looking to the right, our view of the Ionian Sea was blocked by a mountain ridge covered with Holm oaks, heath, myrtle, and lentisk trees.

"Can you hear the voice of the sea?" my grandmother asked me. She knew it was a rhetorical question, because she alone had ears trained to detect the imperceptible sounds of her own past. All I could hear were the harsh cries of swallows overhead and the bands of children coming back from the piazza in the late afternoon. Or Teresa's cheerful voice, as she leaned over the railing of the balcony above us, asking if we wanted to go have a pizza at the beach that evening, with Martina and the rest of the group.

When my parents and Marco arrived, in early July, the real heat had been raging for a week. The village was suffocating under its clammy mantle; people tried to escape its clutches by drinking ice water, wearing as little clothing as possible, closing themselves up in rooms with northern exposures, or, as I did with Martina and our friends, going to the seashore to plunge into the cool waters of, on alternate days, the Tyrrhenian and the Ionian. Only Giorgio Bellusci seemed unaffected by the damp heat, working relentlessly with the now apathetic bricklayers, electricians, and plumbers to finish construction of the Fondaco del Fico. The inauguration was scheduled for the last Saturday in July; it would be open to the public ten days later.

Giorgio Bellusci accorded my parents and my brother just enough time to say hello, drink a cold Coke, and stretch their legs. Half an hour later, he demanded that they take him out to the country in the new Volvo, still loaded with suitcases, because he wanted to show off the Fondaco del Fico. My mother was tired, Marco pretended to be exhausted, Klaus really was wan from the demanding trip—he had done all the driving, and it had been a grueling experience. Next time, he said, he would spend the night in a motel halfway down. Giorgio Bellusci wasn't having any of it. With pleading eyes, my mother entreated Klaus to go along with her father's wishes. I joined the group.

During the drive out to the country, Giorgio Bellusci told my folks that I had met a pretty girl in town named Martina; that we made a nice couple—we went together like pasta and tomato sauce, he said—and that we were so fond of one another that we made love in the open air, standing up, in the park in the middle of the woods.

I felt a hot blush flame across my face. My mother and (what was worse) Marco were laughing unrestrainedly, while my father maintained a faint smile—perhaps he hadn't understood at all. How the hell had the old man heard about this? I had forgotten that in a village this size the trees themselves can spy on you—and tell others everything they see. Even goldfish manage to tell a secret or two. They talk when they should stay quiet, and say nothing when they should be shouting at the top of their gills. Fortunately, Giorgio Bellusci changed the subject: "Florian wants to arrange an exhibition of photographs by Hans on the day of the inauguration. He says that Hans is all for it. He'll arrive in Roccalba with his wife sometime in the next few days."

I saw my father blush like a little boy at this unexpected news.

"Florian is a smart boy," Giorgio Bellusci added. A pat on the head, after the dart he had launched earlier.

That was when we turned off the main road and saw the Fondaco del Fico shimmering in the blast of humid afternoon heat. It looked as if it were suspended in midair, a magical vision that became increasingly concrete as we drew closer.

When we got out of the car, the air was so hot that my tennis shoes stuck to the asphalt that had been laid the day before.

"Allow me to present, ladies and gentlemen, the new Fondaco del Fico," Giorgio Bellusci proclaimed proudly. My parents stood open-mouthed, in patent amazement. They certainly never thought Giorgio Bellusci could actually succeed in creating anything of the sort. Marco was impressed with the light-blue tiles of the swimming pool. There was no water in it. "But in just one week," Giorgio Bellusci said, "the technician is scheduled to come, he'll explain how to work the filter motor and add chlorine and check the levels, and then you can go swimming from morning to night."

Marco was overjoyed, and my mother was giddy as well, as if their bones hadn't just suffered through 2,581 kilometers of highway. My father, on the other hand, trailed around listlessly behind Giorgio Bellusci like a sleepwalker. He barely noticed the wall of ancient stones set like an uncut diamond in the new wall of the main entrance. If there had been beds in the guest rooms we were obliged to tour, he would have laid right down and begun to snore. But the rooms were not yet furnished, the bedrooms and halls were still empty; the balconies were unadorned. "In the next few days the furniture and everything else will be arriving by truck," announced Giorgio Bellusci; he was clearly proud of himself and his stubbornness.

My father finally seemed to wake up fully three days later, once he'd begun to become acclimated. By then, my mother was dragging him around the village to reenact the old ritual of greeting old acquaintances, with that same idiot grin on his lips. I watched Marco panting in the intense heat of late morning, while waiting for my folks to take him to the beach, as promised. I remembered the disastrous summers of my own childhood and, in order to spare him the miseries I experienced at his age, took him to the beach, together with Martina and Teresa.

In the evening, when the vise-grip of humid heat let up, slightly, I would go down to help Giorgio Bellusci. He had to arrange for the inaugural party, hire a band, print the invitations, buy drinks, and decide on the dishes for the buffet.

I knew that Giorgio Bellusci and I, working by ourselves, would never be able to get it all done in time. And so I reached out to Martina, my mother, Teresa, and Aunt Elsa for help, while my father, Uncle Bruno, and even Marco helped Giorgio Bellusci to complete the last little finishing and cleaning jobs. My mother and Martina got to know one another, and they began acting like mother-in-law and daughter-in-law, a little jealous of each other but often in a loose alliance to make fun of me, because I had decided to send a press release to the local press, television, and radio announcing the exhibition of Hans Heumann's photographs. The idea was actually a good one: to exploit the name of a world-famous photographer like Hans Heumann to generate free publicity for the new Fondaco del Fico; that is, I self-corrected, on behalf of a meritorious cause. Martina said that I had delusions of grandeur, just like

Grandpa Giorgio; my mother said over and over that I was just as conceited as Opa Hans. Both of them laughed merrily. Both of them were in love with me.

When Hans Heumann arrived with his wife, two weeks before the inauguration, the Fondaco del Fico was already inhabitable.

"To you goes the honor of deflowering the best room in the house," Giorgio Bellusci told his friend, "but perhaps you have something better in your sights tonight," he added, indicating Hélène with a jut of his chin; fortunately, she missed the lewd reference, and smiled courteously.

Hans and Hélène had just emerged from a red Mercedes convertible, and I was surprised to see how the two old men greeted one another: a simple, friendly handshake, nothing more. I'll admit it: I was expecting an emotional hug, perhaps a tear or two. They hadn't seen each other in fifty years, except for a half-hour visit in a hospital room. They didn't even seem interested in sizing up how the other had changed, after half a century. Or perhaps they were doing their best to conceal their emotions; deep down, maybe, they were weeping with joy.

"Signora, the swimming pool, too, awaits its first swimmer, if you would like to cool off," Giorgio Bellusci said in courtly style to Hélène.

What an old rascal, I thought to myself. Maybe he just wants to see her in a bathing suit! And before the swimming pool could be "deflowered," I jumped in, in shorts and T-shirt. Marco followed suit, after carefully folding his pants and shirt and laying them at the side of the pool.

I was happy. We splashed each other, laughing and spraying water on the others, too; they laughed in genuine amusement, and not just at us: my mother was making repeated but futile attempts to push Klaus into the water; each time she tried, he would ward off her efforts, head down, like a baby goat. We were all happy. Just then, moving quickly, with youthful energy, Hans Heumann went to get one of his cameras from the convertible and began taking photographs, the first ones in a long series. First, pictures of us, in the water, then of the rest of the family, gathered around the pool.

I saw how my father looked fondly into the lens. It melted my heart; he seemed like a child doing everything he could to meet his father's expectations; he put on the obliging smile that I knew all too well, the smile of someone pretending to be good while deeply afraid of others and of life. But there was pride, too, in that smile. Hans saw it and pointed his camera at his son's face, three or four snaps, like loving pats.

That evening, we ate on the terrace that had been built over the old site of the stables. From that height, you could see the reflection of the moon in a small stretch of the sea. "It's really pretty here, very pretty," Hélène kept saying. And my mother nodded in proud agreement, while Giorgio Bellusci answered sarcastically: "Everyone loves this place, and always has; the only ones who don't see its beauty are those who were born here, who live here, and who die here. Here, everyone is blind, and deaf."

"Don't talk like that, it's a sin," my grandmother admonished him. "There are good people here, too, just like anywhere. You were born here yourself, don't forget."

We were finishing up with an iced limoncello when Hélène excused herself from table and went to her bedroom.

Five minutes later she was back; she carried a shiny blue packet, wrapped with a handsome red ribbon. She gave it to Giorgio Bellusci and said, slowly, in Italian: "This our gift for new Fondaco del Fico."

"Best wishes, from the heart," added Hans. And Giorgio Bellusci understood immediately, without opening the packet. First he hugged Hélène, then Hans, at length. Perhaps he wept with his face on his friend's shoulder, for the first time in his life, or perhaps he laughed with joy, at that unexpected surprise, as the scent of bergamot wafted into all our nostrils.

"Thursday, 26 October 1835, 11:30 AM.

"We arrived at this inn about fifteen minutes ago. It is called, if I understood correctly, the *Fundaco del Fico*, a nice name for such a squalid place. We tied up Milord in the stable along with our mounts, else he might have attacked the fat innkeeper just to eat a nice piece of meat. Jadin asked if he could draw a charcoal sketch of the innkeeper and his family, and now the four of them are standing there, as awkward as statues. The two children have their mother's shiny brown eyes; compared with her awkward fat husband, she seems like a delicate flower. In this godforsaken section of Calabria, it is not uncommon to see beautiful women, but you must take care not to look at them even a second too long, or you risk a stiletto in the belly.

"The *pizziota* mule driver warned us, just after we left Pizzo: 'Between here and Maida we will stop at an inn. Take my advice,' he said, 'eat something and then leave in a hurry, don't stop to sleep, for the love of God: in that *Fundaco del Fico* the food is good, but the beds are full of bedbugs and the innkeeper is a friend of the local brigands, who love to rob wayfarers, and occasionally to kill them.'

"As they stand there posing, serious and polite, they don't seem so ferocious and dirty after all. But here in Calabria it is best to trust no one, and I don't even trust the *pizziota*, a man who carries a rifle and wears a bandolier; he already pointed that rifle at someone once, luckily without shooting: it was a beggar in Pizzo who wouldn't stop pleading for charity.

"The innkeeper's son keeps staring at me as I write; it was he who tied up our mounts and Milord in the stable, but first he tried to guess our provenance and destination: 'You are French, aren't you? And you're going to Cosenza, true?' We told him he was right.

"Just a short while ago he brought us drinks. 'This is good wine,' he said. I tasted it. It was grape wine, not wine clumsily diluted with fetid water, as in other inns. 'You are right, it's good,' I answered him. He immediately took a confidential tone. He turned his back to his father, who stood behind the counter, and said to me: 'I want to come with you, if you'll have me.' I smiled at him without answering. 'I know how to do everything,' he said. 'Drive *carriages,* cook, resole shoes, and use a knife better than a criminal.' Around here, the term *carriages* means mules! I said: 'It strikes me that this is a nice place, what more do you want?'

"'I know it's a nice place. I don't want to go away forever, I was born here and I want to die here; I just want to leave for a while, while I'm still young, I want to see the world, go anywhere, as long as it's far from here. Then I'll come back here, to the *Fundaco del Fico*, and when *tata* dies, I'll take his place.'

"I answered him very clearly: 'We don't need anyone.' Partly because I thought of how his father would take it. And since it's a true miracle that we haven't been murdered yet in this adventuresome journey of ours, I certainly don't want to risk my neck for a snotty child. He looked at me with fiery eyes and challenged me: '*Buon viaggio*, Signore,' he said to me, 'the road is long. We'll see one another again soon, and perhaps you'll change your mind then.'

"He went back into the kitchen.

"Now he's back with a plate of macaroni and chickpeas for Jadin—and I feel ill just to look at them—and chestnuts roasted in the embers for me. He's smiling boldly at me. He is tall for a Calabrian, taller than his father. His hair is black and wavy, he has his mother's intelligent expression. He has made signs that he wants to talk to me outside. Later, dear boy, right now I'm as hungry as a wolf."

"What could they have said to each other outside? We'll never know," said my mother, after skillfully translating the page or so that Dumas dedicated to his stop at the Fondaco del Fico. We were having breakfast in my grandparents' house. My mother laid the bergamot-scented album on the table and Giorgio Bellusci, in three precise motions, picked it up, laid it in the wooden box, and shut and locked the lid.

"This young Focubellu really was a restless little character, though, wasn't he?" said my mother.

"A headstrong kid with real balls," Giorgio Bellusci corrected her, and made a vulgar gesture with both hands.

"Of course he was, his name was Giorgio Bellusci," Uncle Bruno observed ironically. Giorgio Bellusci glared at him. Then he turned to me and said: "Let's go to the Fondaco del Fico, to see what that whoremonger Hans Oimànn is up to."

We found Hans Heumann fussing with his camera equipment. He walked toward us. Hélène was still sleeping. Hans Heumann spoke in German: "It is just beautiful here; Hélène is right. We've never slept this well in any hotel we've been in, anywhere on earth. The crickets sang all night long. And then this morning, all the fig trees around here were teeming with birds of all sorts. They were plunging their beaks into the fig skins with such gusto you felt like imitating them. I took a few pictures as soon as I woke up." Then he asked me to translate for him.

"Those damned birds," Giorgio Bellusci responded. "I'll fix them: I'll wrap a nice red ribbon around the foliage of each tree, and they'll be so scared they'll shit themselves the minute there's a breath of wind and the ribbon moves." He burst out laughing with his white teeth, slapped Hans Heumann on the shoulder, and then left him to work undisturbed while he went back into town to buy a ribbon to scare off the birds.

Hans Heumann had brought four cameras with him, all different formats. In the mornings, he would open the windows and look out in ecstasy at the light reflecting off the smooth stones in the dry riverbed. Only a tiny rivulet trickled lazily toward the sea, really just a thread of water wandering around the oleander bushes, heavy with pink flowers. Hans Heumann would select the two cameras he would use all day according to the morning light glinting off the stones; I could never tell the difference. Then he would have breakfast with Hélène on the veranda; later, he would go off, leaving her behind to take the sun and dangle her toes in the water of the swimming pool, while she worked on her tan. He would canvas the area, looking for pictures: in the countryside, along the riverbed, in the village. He would take all the time needed to find a subject worthy of his attention. Sometimes he would come home like a hunter who had found no prey. But when a gaze, a flock of swallows in flight, or the luminous silhouette of a lonely cloud caught his eye, then he would transform his camera into a sort of machine gun.

We would all eat dinner together at my grandparents' house, a huge tableful of food and people, laughter and flavors, a dizzying whirlwind of words in German, Italian, English, Calabrian, and even French, between my mother and Hélène. Giorgio Bellusci would take his immense watermelons out of the refrigerator, place the tip of the knife on the rind, and the watermelons would split in two, with a small thwack that startled Hélène. The incorrigibly gallant Giorgio Bellusci would give her half of the rooster's crest; as a doting grandfather, he'd give the other half of the rooster's crest to Marco. And I realized that the bloody summer of my childhood no longer hurt.

After dinner, we would all go out to the piazza for a lazy gelato, and then to drink a limoncello (or two, or three), sprawled out in the plastic seats in front of the Bar Roma, like a horde of exhausted tourists. Only the two old men had the energy for long walks, arm in arm, tall and slightly stooped, talking animatedly. Who could say what they said to one another? Who could say what they were plotting?

Around midnight I would accompany Hans Heumann and his wife to the Fondaco del Fico, in their Mercedes convertible. I drove, because they weren't used to those roads, full of curves and potholes. And because, after a while, the strong wine that Giorgio Bellusci made and the limoncello took their cumulative toll. You can imagine how excited I was every time I got to step up from driving a Simca to driving a Mercedes convertible; it was like being transformed from a cripple into a long-distance runner, setting a world speed record for the hundred meter dash.

It took about a third of the time to reach the Fondaco del Fico that it did with the Simca. The watchman, whom Giorgio Bellusci had just hired that month, opened the gate, and I would park the Mercedes in front of lame little vehicle, which would then take me slowly back into town, to Martina's sister's house.

A few days before the inauguration, we took a longer trip, all the way to Reggio Calabria, and my excitement rose to the stars. All I had to do was press the accelerator and the car would leap forward, hungry for speed, gobbling the highway miles—and the gasoline—with rude vigor. Next to me was Martina, eyes closed and curls tossing in the wind. Behind us, in comfortable leather seats, Hélène and Hans were cooing like newlyweds on their honeymoon. They were relaxed, almost too relaxed, in a way; they were kissing and laughing.

Hans Heumann had a photographer friend in Reggio Calabria who would lend him his darkroom for the day. The idea was to develop the film and select twenty or so photographs to add to the old pictures, already printed, to tell the story of the Fondaco del Fico, said Hans Heumann in English, and evading the compliment when I said that it seemed like a great idea.

The photographer was a man with wavy grey hair, younger than Hans Heumann and, apparently, well known in the field of photography. To me, his name—Giosuè Girardi—meant nothing. He had a studio downtown. He offered us iced coffee, and then Hélène, Martina, and I took a stroll around the city. Hans Heumann would be busy until late that night.

As we strolled along the waterfront, Martina took my hand. Hélène began walking on ahead, putting on speed and sniffing the air, scented with orange blossoms, making comments on the Art Nouveau villas, admiring the palm trees and the flowering agaves. We couldn't keep up with her. She seemed like a speedwalker trying to win a race. People turned to watch her go by, especially the men. And you certainly don't see a tall, beautiful woman like Hélène, with the figure of a model, every day, not even in a city full of beautiful women like Reggio Calabria. I told Martina that I felt like yelling out: "Gentlemen, this is my grandmother!" I could just imagine the reaction. They'd think I was insane. And Martina pointed out that my face was already distraught, from the heat and the sweat; I already looked pretty crazy. It was true: I wanted to rest and cool my head under an open faucet.

The photographer, Girardi had recommended we make sure to see the bronze Warriors of Riace. After we had a leisurely lunch in a restaurant overlooking the water, we walked over to the National Museum. The rapt gazes of

Hélène and Martina doubled, through contact, my immense admiration for the two perfect statues; it seemed as if you could see the blood running through the veins on their arms and hands.

We told Hans Heumann about what we had experienced, when we went to pick him up, but he ignored us. In fact, he asked us if we could go take another stroll around town, and get some dinner, because he had hours of darkroom work ahead of him. He was grumpy, nervous, and sweaty.

As we had agreed, we stayed away until one in the morning. He was exhausted. "The photographs are almost ready for the show," he said. "Giosuè Girardi will bring them to Roccalba. I wish I had had more time, to proof and print: they're all right, but nothing special."

He fell asleep as soon as I turned onto the highway.

I thought the photos were magnificent. And to listen to their comments, the crowd that showed up at the Fondaco del Fico for the inauguration liked them, too; the people were from Roccalba and the surrounding area. The pictures were an epilogue, partly in color, of a story that began with a photographic enlargement of Jadin's black-on-white sketch. The photographs that Hans took during his youthful journey took on an epic aura after fifty years, like anything from the past seen through loving eyes. Dominating the show was the photograph of Giorgio Bellusci with the long hair of a savage, the dog Milord at his feet, standing in front of the cavity-ridden dinosaur incisor called Fondaco del Fico.

One after another, three television news crews arrived and began filming.

The show had been installed in an unusual setting: the first photographs that visitors saw hung from the branches of the trees in the hotel garden, dangling from little chrome-plated brass chains; the slightest breeze would make them swing. Other pictures stood on painter's easels or were hung on the white walls of the Fondaco del Fico.

The crowd followed the twists and turns of the installation, and wound all the way around the hotel. Looking down from the sun porch, on the top floor, it seemed like a black curl moving slowly, being sucked into the main doorway, but never entirely.

Inside, Giosuè Girardi was waiting impatiently to perform

the "very thankful task," as he put it, of presenting the work of Hans Heumann. Starting with the pictures in the hall, he pointed out that the exhibition focused on clear contrasts and comparisons, rather than taking a chronological approach. And so, next to the photograph of the head of the savage young Bellusci, you could admire a photograph of the old Bellusci baring his white teeth in a ferocious laugh, while his sunburnt-brown eyes, the eyes that Hans liked so much, followed you in all directions, wherever you moved, like the eyes of the Mona Lisa.

Giosuè Girardi then talked about Hans Heumann's ability to tell a story in a single photograph, and his ironic and, at the same time, bitter gaze on life. He showed great expertise and, at the same time, sincere admiration for his friend, but also a very limited understanding of his audience, who understood little or nothing of those abstruse concepts, nor of comparisons to Cartier-Bresson's "stolen images"—some of the people listening assumed this Cartier-Bresson was a thief. But the audience was patient, and whenever he referred to Hans Heumann as "one of the greatest photographers on earth," they applauded loud and long.

Fortunately Hans Heumann understood that people were interested in pictures, but not words. So when he was asked to speak, he limited himself to three observations in a strangely grammatical and fluent Italian: "I had prepared a thirty-page lecture to explain my art to you, but my friend Giosuè stole it from me, and I thank him from the bottom of my heart." Fake laughter. "I would like to add just one phrase from Robert Frank, a photographer friend of mine: 'I have a lot in back of me—of what has happened in my life—and that's a tremendous pull backward. And in front of me I love the sea.'"

And we all looked in the direction that Hans was looking, and we saw it, the sea, covered by a translucent haze of muggy heat, a thin line just a little darker than the sky, which hypnotized us until Hans began to speak again. "One last thing, and a very important one, the important thing of all: Giorgio is a great man, and he has a special spumante, let's all go drink a toast, I'm thirsty."

In an instant, the cloak of seriousness that Giosuè Girardi had lowered over the event was torn to shreds by an enthusiastic ovation and a round of laughter. Only my father remained serious: he walked over to Hans and, shaking his hand, told him how much he liked the show. Then we all went out into the garden for a drink, while waiting for the official inauguration of the Fondaco del Fico, scheduled for seven o'clock.

When Giorgio Bellusci's turn came, the television cameras had been turned off long ago, but there were twice as many people there to listen to him, and women, men, and children continued to come in.

"Just a couple of words," began Giorgio Bellusci in a voice throbbing with emotion. "Let me begin by thanking you all, for your love, a thank-you to my family, who have helped me through the hardest times. A thank-you to Hans for his help with money and his magnificent photographs, which put a cherry on top of this delicious cake. Without Hans, we wouldn't even be here to celebrate today. My last thank-you goes to my grandson Florian, who has been a huge help to me recently. I will entrust the Fondaco del Fico to him, soon, when I am gone, up there, looking down on you all with them." And he pointed to the swallows swooping overhead, while the crowd roared: "In a hundred years, in a hundred years.

"Well, I don't feel old, that's true, but I am. I am entrusting this place to him, and to the future. Because, certainly you have all understood this: none of these sacrifices were for me, to make me famous or respected. I did all this for us, for the future of this beautiful land of ours, this land that Hans's photographs show so well, this land that someone—and you all know who I mean—is trying to destroy."

For an instant, everyone fell silent, even the children; perhaps everyone was holding their breath. It was as if Giorgio Bellusci had just mentioned the Devil. A number of old women almost crossed themselves. Just then, a car roared into the Fondaco del Fico, tires squealing. Two tall and athletic young men wearing sunglasses bounded out of the car. The crowd stared at them, petrified. Someone actually turned to run, so tense was the moment. Then a massive, stoop-shouldered man got out, made his way through the crowd, and went over to hug Giorgio Bellusci and shake Hans Heumann's hand. Many people recognized him: it was the president of the province. The television cameras began to roll again.

"Forgive me for arriving late," said the president, "and for interrupting. I'll be very brief. I am here to convey the greetings and best wishes of the provincial assembly, and my own. To have rebuilt, with such determination, a piece of our local history was a meritorious undertaking. I sincerely hope that the Fondaco del Fico can serve as a spur for development in new directions, for strategic planning for the future . . ." And he went on talking for another fifteen minutes, drawing three rounds of applause. "Thank you! I have nothing more to say," he added after a calculated pause. "Let the party continue!" And he did his best to blend in with the crowd, in vain. There was a last, liberating burst of applause, and the crowd began to laugh and joke. Giorgio Bellusci cried: "The bottle to me!"

A bottle of spumante dangling from a length of cord descended, as if by enchantment, from a third-story balcony.

Giorgio Bellusci grabbed it with one hand and then hurled it, with all the strength he could muster, against the ancient stone core of the Fondaco del Fico. The bottle shattered with a sharp crack; it left a broad wet stain on the stones, at the exact place where a small fig tree once grew, but had been blown to bits.

Immediately after that, the band began to play and sing cheerful songs, and a number of couples began dancing. The banquet tables, crowded with cold dishes like prosciutto, cheeses, pickled vegetables, slices of mortadella and sausage and *soppressata* salami, *nduja* creamy sausage, *pizzette*, squash-blossom fritters, sardelles, sardines stuffed with pecorino cheese and parsley, cold lasagna, veal stew, and watermelon and canteloupe slices, were attacked and cleaned better than an army of starving mice could have done.

It was a memorable party. For the first time in my life, I saw my parents dance, moving close together like young lovers. Hans danced with my grandmother, Hélène danced with Giorgio Bellusci, and Marco danced with Aunt Elsa, Teresa with Uncle Bruno. Martina held my hand, proud of what *zu* Giorgio had said about me, while I had not yet realized the scale of the responsibility that had just dropped onto my shoulders.

That evening I met Martina's sister. She had just come down from Switzerland with her husband and children a couple of days before, so we wouldn't be able to use her house. What did I care? I had the keys to every room in the Fondaco del Fico.

The first one to leave was the president, with a send-off of applause and a few scornful whistles, as the tires of his automobile squealed needlessly. Then families with small children left; finally—at three in the morning—young people left, and Martina said good night.

"There have never been so many guests at a party," said Giorgio Bellusci proudly, and then wrapped an arm around his wife's soft shoulders.

FOURTH JOURNEY

T wo days after the inauguration, Hans, Hélène, and—an unannounced surprise—Giorgio Bellusci all left together. That morning, we all had breakfast together, at my grandparents' house: ricotta cake, freshly baked bread with fig marmalade, coffee and blood-red mulberry juice. Giorgio Bellusci ate with gusto and then he tossed me the heavy ring of keys to the Fondaco del Fico. "Youngster, I've done what I needed to do, now it's your turn. There are the keys to the chest of drawers and to the wooden box, too!" That was it. Not another word. Only a long thuggish gaze that I didn't understand and I couldn't hold.

First stop, Lamezia airport, where Hélène would catch an 11:50 flight for Rome, and a connection from there to Paris: she had a lot of business to take care of. Then the two men would continue alone. They wanted to relive, more or less, the trip they had taken fifty years before, in the red VW Beetle.

They were happy and relaxed, as if leaving on a pleasure trip. My mother told them to have fun. Klaus and Marco smiled and waved goodbye. Only my grandmother said: "Be careful, please, be careful."

I caught Martina's eye in the small crowd of relatives and friends, clustering around the car in a giant embrace. She has unforgettable eyes, the deep green of Holm oaks. Martina gave me a conspiratorial wink, a *zingatella*, as she calls it, and in an instant I was transported back to our night in the Fondaco del Fico, the last kiss, so long and drawn out my lips were still burning. She said to me at the time: "Let them go by themselves." My grandfathers wanted to take me with them, for a few days. I replied, uncertainly: "It seems like a once-in-a-lifetime opportunity to get to know them better, to get to know this land." She was positive: "Don't you see? This is their journey. You wouldn't fit in. And then, if you stay here, you'll get to know me better." I smiled at her with my burning lips and turned out the light.

Now, as I watched them leave, I felt a burst of regret warm my cheeks, along with the heat of the summer day. It was the twenty-seventh of July, and the muggy heat clung to the skin like hot glue.

Hélène hit the horn twice: the bright clear, loud sound cleared the black swarm of swallows from the sky. It all happened in an instant. Dozens of women leaned out of the windows, a small cluster of men came out of the bar. Hélène put the car into first gear and the car moved away slowly. The swallows came back, diving and soaring, tireless.

We know for certain that Hélène drove as far as Lamezia, and we know for sure that the two men told each other stories of that legendary journey, and laughed all the way. As they said goodbye, they told her that they would be back in two weeks, no longer than that, and anyway that she shouldn't worry, they were adults and they knew how to take care of themselves. "Ah, don't think that we're a couple of nostalgic old men," Hans added. "We just want to fill our eyes with beautiful images. And our bellies with delicious food and good wine, right, Giorgio? And take a few pictures, like on our first trip."

Giorgio Bellusci had nodded, serious, his eyes glowing with sunlight.

In the first photograph, Hélène is boarding the aircraft: she has a hand on her lips; perhaps she was blowing a kiss to the two men, already far away.

From Lamezia, Hans drove, "because I would lend Giorgio anything," he had said it many times before, "even my heart, but my car and my wife no, never, I don't trust you, dear Giorgio, you would destroy them both in a minute."

The second stop was at Pizzo Calabro. Or at least, that was where Hans began taking pictures again; first the castle, where Murat had been held prisoner, then the sea from the belvedere in the main piazza, while Giorgio licked a gelato, his eyes almost closed. A short while later, at the table in the *gelateria*, they wrote their first postcard.

"Caro Florian, a fond hello from Pizzo. Here they make the best gelato on earth. We ate an extra gelato for you. It's too bad you didn't come, we miss you, but a pretty *cervella* is more important than two old jerks. We wouldn't have done any different if we were in your place. A kiss to everyone. Giorgio and Hans."

Then they drove south toward Reggio, they followed the Costa Viola for a stretch and, perhaps from Monte Sant'Elia, Hans photographed the silhouettes of Mount Etna and the Aeolian Isles in the reddish glow of sunset. They reached Scilla around ten at night. They ate dinner and slept in a hotel near the harbor.

Hans took more pictures at dawn: a slice of Sicily lost in the sea, an old woman combing her stringy hair in a village alley, a solitary seagull flying over the empty beach. When he came back to the hotel, Giorgio Bellusci was still asleep: Hans photographed him in bed, covered with a sheet up to his neck, eyes shut, arms at his sides, like a dead man.

"Caro Florian, Scilla is beautiful. You should come here with Martina. It's as if you could reach out and touch one of Sicily's horns. There is a pensione, just a few steps from the

Spiaggia delle Sirene, where they serve raw swordfish carpaccio, marinated in bergamot juice. When you finish, you want to order another. A hug to everyone. Hans and Giorgio."

Giorgio was hale and healthy for the rest of the journey; he talked, but we don't know what he said. He gesticulated like my mother.

They reached the bottom of the toe of the Italian boot, not far from Cape Spartivento, and tried to find an abandoned garden, between state road 106 and the sea. They both remembered it clearly—it was a tangled labyrinth of bergamot orange trees and jasmine vines, citron trees and orange blossoms, lemon trees and tangerine trees, a wafting concert of scents that would bring a dead man to life—they had found it by following their noses. But now they couldn't find it. Nearby, construction was underway on a tourist resort; next to it was a small campground with dusty, twisted eucalyptus trees.

Disappointed, they started up the road along the slope of the escarpment facing the Ionian Sea. The villages are perched on cliff sides.

Every so often, they would stop by the side of the road to relieve themselves. From up there, looking down would make your head spin. The beaches crawled with sunbathers and beach umbrellas, the coastline was encrusted with cement and construction sites, villas large and small, campgrounds and the occasional hotel. The towns along the coast are long rows of houses, and beyond is nothing but the cobalt blue of the sea.

They parked the car in the parking lot of a restaurant-hotel and walked quickly up a steep trail through chestnut groves.

"Caro Florian, we saw the Fondaco del Fico from the Serra Alta: it looks like a ship on a green and yellow sea. The two real seas, on either side, look like a pair of blue eyes, with white foam-topped waves. I can't wait to develop the pictures. A kiss from Giorgio, too. Yours, Hans."

The next day, they traveled along the Strada dei Due Mari—the Two Seas Road—toward Catanzaro. They didn't notice the motorcycle following them. How could they? They looked at the landscape with the eyes of lovers. Hans was fascinated by the glittering white stones in a dry riverbed and the oleanders that grew, healthy and vigorous, along the same riverbed, without a drop of water. They never looked in the rear-view mirrors.

They drove north along the Ionian coast until they reached Le Castella; they took a swim there to cool off. The sea was warm and crystal clear; the shoals of tiny anchovies were gleaming banks of light; they dried off on a huge hot rock. Seen from there, the castle in the water seemed as if it were flying through the light blue of sea and sky.

Then they drove along a short stretch of coastline to the north, until they reached Cape Colonna. Here Hans shot pictures as if he were firing a machine gun. The best one shows Giorgio standing before the last surviving column of the temple of Hera Lacinia; his face is filled with vivid shadow and light. Behind him, the sea is glowing with sunlight.

At midday, they ate in Crotone, at Casa di Rosa, tagliatelle with salted grouper, baked mussels, and a nice mixed seafood au gratin. They drank three bottles of Cirò wine; they were tipsy and happy.

They left Crotone in the afternoon, driving into a blinding sun, past two decrepit abandoned factories at the outskirts of town. A short distance further on, they took the superhighway for Cosenza and stopped at San Giovanni in Fiore, the town where Giorgio's mother was born and raised. They looked around for a nice local restaurant and a place to sleep. Then they strolled around the town. Perhaps at Giorgio's instigation,

Hans photographed a number of girls, most of them unawares, others smiling for the camera. They all have black, gleaming eyes, and long wavy hair; they really are pretty, and they deserve their reputation for beauty.

They woke up very early the next morning, because Hans wanted to stop and do some landscape photography in the Sila. They drank cold water from a stream running down a slope covered with ferns; the water poured into Giorgio's open mouth and trickled down his chin.

They drank their last espresso in Camigliatello. They wrote a hasty postcard and left. The motorcycle pulled out behind them.

Later, from a high plaza with a scenic overlook, directly above a terrifying drop and then, further out, a view of the entire Crati river valley and the city of Cosenza sleeping under a blanket of humid heat, Hans took just two photographs: a foreshortened view of the roofs down below, with swallows flying above them, looking as big as eagles from this point of view, and a closeup of Giorgio with a sudden flare of rage, or perhaps fear, in his sunburnt-brown eyes. He had seen the two men coming up behind Hans, there is no doubt about it. He didn't have time even to open his mouth, to make an effort to defend himself, or try to get away: the two men shot him in the face with six bullets from a 7.65-mm. caliber pistol, extinguishing for all time that thuggish glare.

Hans? Hans was certainly trembling. He knew that he had nothing to do with all this; he loved the light and the colors of this land, he even loved the muggy heat that makes you feel drunk. He hoped they might let him live. It only took a few seconds. He saw his friend crumple over the fender of the Mercedes, his face torn to shreds, and then he screamed out his grief and rage, he screamed in his language incomprehensible words of anger, until one of the two men hit him in the temple with the butt of the pistol. They didn't even waste bullets on Hans; they just put him in the car, behind the wheel, and laid Giorgio next to him, both belted in. Then they pushed the Mercedes out into the void.

"Caro Florian, we're doing fine. We both feel years younger. But we miss Milord. Best wishes for the opening of the Fondaco del Fico. We'll be thinking of you. We're going to continue our journey. A kiss to everyone. Hans and Giorgio."

A Stay at the Fondaco del Fico

When you asked me if I knew that Alexandre Dumas had stopped at the old Fondaco del Fico, I knew you weren't just an ordinary tourist.

You pelted me with questions about Giorgio Bellusci, Hans Heumann, and my parents; it was only after a few days that you told me anything about yourself. You admitted you were a writer and that you had spent many summers searching for the Fondaco del Fico. And so I understood why you were traveling around with that air of a detective trying to pass himself off as a tourist. You look for a place, and what you find is stories. That's how Dumas worked, too, isn't it?

I don't know if my jumbled memories can be of any help to you; I know that it has helped me to remember. And by remembering, it seemed to help me understand better people who were very dear to me.

With the passage of time, my mother recovered. During the summers she comes to see me, with Klaus and Marco, and they help me out. My grandmother, instead, aged ten years in a single day, and now she only talks to the sea, dragging herself through the house like a phantom. My mother, on the other hand, doesn't neglect her appearance, in spite of everything that happened. She dyes her hair black, she uses a pound of blush to cover her wrinkles. My mother is still beautiful. I don't know where she finds the strength to recover, when all these catastrophes knock her to the floor. "I only have one worry now," she says, "and that is you."

No, she's not relaxed. Though no one has ever stopped by to ask for a payoff, to offer their "protection." For that matter, they know perfectly well how much money I'm making. "They wouldn't waste time with you," Avvocato Arcuri reassured me. He has a thriving law office in the city, and whenever he's in Roccalba he stops by to say hello. "They have their drug traffic to manage," he said, "they need to run illegal immigrants, get contracts for major public-works projects, and shake down big corporations."

But I'm here, claws out, I'm not lowering my guard. The whole village, or nearly, is on my side.

I spend four months of the year in my other home, in Hamburg, where I was born. I need it, to keep from losing bits of my past and maybe my future. Living in two places as different from one another as the sun and the moon, it seems as if I'm living two lives; each place I go, I dive in headfirst. Living on the surface isn't my way.

No, I keep the Fondaco del Fico open in the nice weather, from March to October. In July and August, we're full to bursting, as you've seen, because of the pool, so that people don't miss the beach too much. Though anyone who wants to can hop in the car and be down on the Tyrrhenian beaches in fifteen minutes, or the Ionian beaches in a little over a half-hour. And groups of young people come down from Roccalba and other towns around here, almost every evening, to eat here. Sometimes, a dusty, solitary traveler will spend the night. Foreigners, perhaps, or Italians, I couldn't say. Nowadays, the differences are almost imperceptible.

But there was something familiar about you, as if I had met you before somewhere, who can say when. Or maybe it was just the way you talked about the Fondaco del Fico, as if it belonged to you, too, as if you were a member of the family.

When you went back to your room, I said in jest to Martina: "He has a round face and a dimple on his chin, just like

Dumas, this man." And she replied, playing along with the joke:

"The same frizzy hair, just not as thick. Yes, perhaps it's the ghost of Alexandre Dumas who has come to take back his album." I told her not to worry, because the album is safe in a hidden wooden box, along with Jadin's sketch. We are saving them for our children, when they arrive.

We laughed at our wild fantasies. But we weren't far off the mark. You writers all look the same. You all have the same eyes of insatiable vampires.

And now farewell, my friend, for I have nothing left to tell you. Let me finish with a final piece of news, a piece of good news: on the twenty-fourth of October, Martina and I are getting married. We'll have a big party, here, at the Fondaco del Fico.

The Days of Abandonment
Elena Ferrante
Fiction - 192 pp - $14.95 - isbn 978-1-933372-00-6

"Stunning . . . The raging, torrential voice of the author is something rare."—*The New York Times*

"I could not put this novel down. Elena Ferrante will blow you away."—ALICE SEBOLD, author of *The Lovely Bones*

This gripping story tells of a woman's descent into devastating emptiness after being abandoned by her husband with two young children to care for.

Troubling Love
Elena Ferrante
Fiction - 144 pp - $14.95 - isbn 978-1-933372-16-7

"In tactile, beautifully restrained prose, Ferrante makes the domestic violence that tore [the protagonist's] household apart evident."—*Publishers Weekly*

"Ferrante has written the 'Great Neapolitan Novel.'"
—*Corriere della Sera*

Delia's takes a voyage of discovery through the chaotic streets and claustrophobic sitting rooms of contemporary Naples in search of the truth about her mother's untimely death.

Cooking with Fernet Branca
James Hamilton-Paterson
Fiction - 288 pp - $14.95 - isbn 978-1-933372-01-3

"Provokes the sort of indecorous involuntary laughter that has more in common with sneezing than chuckling. Imagine a British John Waters crossed with David Sedaris."—*The New York Times*

Gerald Samper has his own private Tuscan hilltop, where he whiles away his time working as a ghostwriter for celebrities and inventing wholly original culinary concoctions. His idyll is shattered by the arrival of Marta. A series of hilarious misunderstandings brings this odd couple into ever-closer proximity.

Old Filth
Jane Gardam
Fiction - 256 pp - $14.95 - isbn 978-1-933372-13-6

"This remarkable novel [...] will bring immense pleasure to readers who treasure fiction that is intelligent, witty, sophisticated and—a quality encountered all too rarely in contemporary culture—adult."—*The Washington Post*

The engrossing and moving account of the life of Sir Edward Feathers; from birth in colonial Malaya to Wales, where he is sent as a "Raj orphan," to Oxford, his career and marriage parallels much of the twentieth century's dramatic history.

Total Chaos
Jean-Claude Izzo
Fiction/Noir - 256 pp - $14.95 - isbn 978-1-933372-04-4

"Rich, ambitious and passionate . . . his sad, loving portrait of his native city is amazing."—*The Washington Post*

"Full of fascinating characters, tersely brought to life in a prose style that is (thanks to Howard Curtis's shrewd translation) traditionally dark and completely original."—*The Chicago Tribune*

The first installment in the Marseilles Trilogy.

Chourmo
Jean-Claude Izzo
Fiction/Noir - 256 pp - $14.95 - isbn 978-1-933372-17-4

"Like the best noir writers—and he is among the best—Izzo not only has a keen eye for detail but also digs deep into what makes men weep."—*Time Out New York*

Fabio Montale is dragged back into the mean streets of a violent, crime-infested Marseilles after the disappearance of his long-lost cousin's teenage son.

The Goodbye Kiss
Massimo Carlotto
Fiction/Noir - 192 pp - $14.95 - isbn 978-1-933372-05-1

"A nasty, explosive little tome warmly recommended to fans of James M. Cain for its casual amorality and truly astonishing speed."—*Kirkus Reviews*

An unscrupulous womanizer, as devoid of morals now as he once was full of idealistic fervor, returns to Italy, where he is wanted for a series of crimes. To avoid prison he sells out his old friends, turns his back on his former ideals and cuts deals with crooked cops. To earn himself the guise of respectability he is willing to go even further, maybe even as far as murder.

www.europaeditions.com

Death's Dark Abyss
Massimo Carlotto
Fiction/Noir - 192 pp - $14.95 - isbn 978-1-933372-18-1

"A narrative voice that in Lawrence Venuti's translation is cold and heartless—but, in a creepy way, fascinating."—*The New York Times*

A riveting drama of guilt, revenge, and justice, Massimo Carlotto's *Death's Dark Abyss* tells the story of two men and the savage crime that binds them. During a robbery, Raffaello Beggiato takes a young woman and her child hostage and later murders them. Beggiato is arrested, tried, and sentenced to life. The victims' father and husband, Silvano, plunges into a deepening abyss until the day the murderer seeks his pardon and he begins to plot his revenge.

Hangover Square
Patrick Hamilton
Fiction/Noir - 280 pp - $14.95 - isbn 978-1-933372-06-8

"Hamilton is a sort of urban Thomas Hardy: always a pleasure to read, and as social historian he is unparalleled."—NICK HORNBY

Adrift in the grimy pubs of London at the outbreak of World War II, George Harvey Bone is hopelessly infatuated with Netta, a cold, contemptuous small-time actress. George also suffers from occasional blackouts. During these moments one thing is horribly clear: he must murder Netta.

www.europaeditions.com

Boot Tracks
Matthew F. Jones
Fiction/Noir - 208 pp - $14.95 - isbn 978-1-933372-11-2

"More than just a very good crime thriller, this dark but illuminating novel shows us the psychopathology of the criminal mind . . . A nightmare thriller with the power to haunt."
—*Kirkus Reviews* (starred)

A commanding, stylishly written novel that tells the harrowing story of an assassination gone terribly wrong and the man and woman who are taking their last chance to find a safe place in a hostile world.

Love Burns
Edna Mazya
Fiction/Noir - 192 pp - $14.95 - isbn 978-1-933372-08-2

"This book, which has Woody Allen overtones, should be of great
interest to readers of black humor and psychological thrillers."
—*Library Journal* (starred)

Ilan, a middle-aged professor of astrophysics, discovers that his
young wife is having an affair. Terrified of losing her, he decides to
confront her lover instead. Their meeting ends in the latter's
murder—the unlikely murder weapon being Ilan's pipe—and in
desperation, Ilan disposes of the body in the fresh grave of his
kindergarten teacher. But when the body is discovered, the
mayhem begins.

Departure Lounge
Chad Taylor
Fiction/Noir - 176 pp - $14.95 - isbn 978-1-933372-09-9

"Smart, original, surprising and just about as cool as a novel can get . . . Taylor can flat out write."—*The Washington Post*

A young woman mysteriously disappears. The lives of those she has left behind—family, acquaintances, and strangers intrigued by her disappearance—intersect to form a captivating latticework of coincidences and surprising twists of fate. Urban noir at its stylish and intelligent best.